The Country of Herself

The Country of Herself

Short Fiction by Chicago Women

Karen Lee Osborne, editor

Chicago

Design and production by Midge Stocker

Printed on recycled, acid-free paper in the United States of America.

We gratefully acknowledge the following for permission to reprint previously published work:

Mary Gray Hughes, "The Foreigner in the Blood": from *The Calling*. Copyright © 1980 by Mary Gray Hughes. Reprinted by permission of the author and the University of Illinois Press.

Patricia Lear, "Angels": from *Stardust, 7-Eleven, Route 57, A & W, And So Forth*. Copyright © 1992 by Patricia Lear. Reprinted by permission of the author and Alfred A. Knopf, Inc.

Maxine Chernoff, "The Stockholm Syndrome": from *Story*, winter 1990. Copyright © 1990 by Maxine Chernoff. Also reprinted in *Signs of Devotion*, published by Simon and Schuster. Reprinted by permission of the author.

Eleanore Devine, "I Miss Saturday Night": from *Other Voices* 16 (spring 1992). Copyright © 1992 by Eleanore Devine. Reprinted by permission of the author.

Anne Brashler, "Vibrations Which Rumble Like Thunder": from *Getting Jesus in the Mood*. Copyright © 1991 by Anne Brashler. Reprinted by permission of the author and Cane Hill Press.

Joyce Goldenstern, "A Slight Movement of Hands": from *Primavera*. Copyright © 1987 by Joyce Goldenstern. Reprinted by permission of the author.

June Rachuy Brindel, "Service": from *Nobody Is Ever Missing*, published by Story Press. Copyright © 1984 by June Rachuy Brindel. Reprinted by permission of the author.

Sara Paretsky, "The Man Who Loved Life": from *New Chicago Stories*, published by City Stoop Press. Copyright © 1990 by Sara Paretsky. Reprinted by permission of the author.

S. L. Wisenberg, "My Mother's War": from *Another Chicago Magazine* 16. Copyright © 1986 by S. L. Wisenberg. Reprinted by permission of the author.

Sharon Solwitz, "The Country of Herself": from *The Chicago Tribune*. Copyright © 1992 by Sharon Solwitz. Reprinted by permission of the author.

Library of Congress Cataloging-in-Publication Data
The Country of herself : short fiction / by Chicago women ; Karen Lee
  Osborne, editor. —1st ed.
    p.   cm.
    ISBN 1-879427-14-1 (pbk. : alkl. paper)
    1. Short stories, American—Illinois—Chicago. 2. Short stories,
American—Women authors. 3. Women—Illinois—Chicago—Fiction.
4. American fiction—20th century. 5. Chicago (Ill.)—Fiction.
I. Osborne, Karen Lee, 1954-
PS572.C5C68   1993
813'.01089287—dc20   93-28677
                                                               CIP

This book is available on tape to disabled women from the Womyn's Braille Press, P.O. Box 8475, Minneapolis, MN 55408.

                              Third Side Press
                              2250 W. Farragut
                              Chicago, IL 60625-1802

First edition, October 1993
10 9 8 7 6 5 4 3 2 1

Contents

Acknowledgments

The editor wishes to thank Cynthia Cappello and JoAnn Ziebarth for their valuable assistance in the preparation of this collection. A special thanks goes to Fred Shafer for sharing his knowledge and wisdom.

Introduction

This anthology of short fiction pays special attention to women writers. The theme and title are derived from Sharon Solwitz's contribution, "The Country of Herself." All of these stories examine, in divergent ways, the theme of self and other. Some of these stories take us to different countries. In others, familiar territory is transformed by discoveries of unfamiliar truths. While most of the stories have female protagonists, two of the stories are written from the perspective of a male protagonist, and a third uses alternating points of view, a husband's and a wife's. All of these characters speak with voices that command attention, in cadences that ring true.

By the time I moved to Chicago in 1986, the year my first novel was published by Academy Chicago, I had already read and admired works by some of the contributors to this collection. As a writer, a teacher, and a lifelong student of literature, I am nourished by the powerful work my fellow Chicagoans are producing. A desire to celebrate the work of Chicago writers prompted me to cofound City Stoop Press in 1990 with two colleagues. In three anthologies of Chicago writing, *New Chicago Stories, West Side Stories*, and *South Side Stories*, City Stoop brought together the

works of both established and emerging Chicago
fiction writers. Several other anthologies of Chicago
writing in the past decade, including the 1984
TriQuarterly multi-genre compilation and the 1990
Chicago Works, document the literary renaissance
flourishing here. A collection of women's poetry and
fiction, *Naming the Daytime Moon*, was published in
1986 by the Feminist Writers Guild and subsequently
reissued by Another Chicago Press. The *Nommo*
anthologies, the most recent of which appeared in
1992, have showcased the work of prominent and
emerging African-American Chicago writers. It is my
hope that readers curious about Chicago writers will
investigate all of these texts, for each contains valuable work.

There is enough powerful storytelling in *The Country of Herself: Short Fiction by Chicago Women* to entice any reader. If you've ever heard Angela Jackson
read her poetry or prose aloud, you know how electri-
fying a presence she is, and her linguistic and oratori-
cal magic energizes "The Island of the Rooster."
Regina, the narrator, has gone to an unnamed Caribbean island that resembles Haiti. Preoccupied with her
love for the enigmatic Will, frustrated with his inscru-
table nature, haunted by her urge for pregnancy, she
seeks out a voodoo priestess. Although Will is quick
to point out the connection between superstition and
oppression, Regina does find a kind of magic in an island woman's transcendent love for her baby daughter.

One need not go abroad to encounter what seems
foreign in others or in the self. Perhaps the most disturbing of such encounters is the reality of growing
old and losing one's identity. In Mary Gray Hughes's
classic story "The Foreigner in the Blood," the analyst
Leon Esteban is famous for, among other things, his
published work on senility. Now his daughter Clara,
also a psychiatrist, must face the descent of her promi-

nent father into the very senility he has described. The story opens and closes with the image of a mirror. At the beginning, Esteban looks into a mirror and does not recognize the strange man he sees there. The story ends with Esteban watching himself intently in the mirror, convinced he is being watched by millions on a television program. The father Clara once knew is lost and has been replaced with someone she does not know. When she takes him to a mountainside park, its steep terrain is nothing compared to the frightening territory of her father's illness.

Several stories blend humor with this theme of situating the self in an unfamiliar context. In Patricia Lear's "Angels," an unlikely handyman wearing a Louis Vuitton purse accompanies his convalescing female employer to a department store, where they frolic in makeup and lingerie, defying death. "Angels" reveals a good deal more than its surface details. Like "The Foreigner in the Blood," it looks the unpleasant in the eye and doesn't blink. Vernon, the handyman, does a great deal more for his employer than drive her to a store; he helps her to remember that although she has had cancer, she is alive.

Maxine Chernoff's "The Stockholm Syndrome" also plays with deceptive appearances. The narrator and her friend are full of snap judgments about an unconventional friend and her unconventional son, but they encounter a few surprises, and happily revise some silly misconceptions about marital status and sexuality. Eleanore Devine, in "I Miss Saturday Night," challenges stereotypes with humor while exploring the realities of aging. The irreverent narrator is quite in charge of her identity and her soul, while her fast-track daughter and son-in-law seem to be the strict fuddy-duddies in danger of losing theirs.

Women can lose their identities by becoming subsumed in relationships with their husbands, their mothers, their daughters, or even strangers. In "Vibrations Which Rumble Like Thunder" by Anne Brashler, two couples nearly exchange identities when they trade houses, a matter described with sharp wit. The *doppelganger* Mrs. Polanski's real offense lies not in adopting the style and brand of clothing the narrator wears, but in looking better in them than the narrator does. "This was not a friendly neighbor asking about a wicker chair or a framed print. Mr. and Mrs. Polanski swallowed people whole." The narrator, who feels she has "lost part of herself," reasserts her will through self-transformation and encourages her husband Darly to reclaim his identity. The story ends with an image of Darly's small circus, his means of enchanting and entertaining others.

Such references to mirrors, magic, illusion, and performance, especially as they pertain to self-knowledge and self-deception, recur throughout *The Country of Herself*. In Joyce Goldenstern's "A Slight Movement of Hands," the narrator's Uncle Gabriel entertains and charms his way into the hearts of children and adults. The young narrator tries very hard to dislike Gabriel because she knows that he's an adulterer and that this is wrong. Yet it's not so easy. She sees through his performances, his tricks, but his affectionate nature is genuine, and the magician himself is not immune to changes beyond his control.

Facing situations beyond one's control is the subject of Diane Williams's story, where the *doppelganger* device is again used effectively. Kerry, the female cab driver of "In Kerry's Cab," looks in her rearview mirror and sees a woman who should be a "sister" but who becomes her nemesis instead. Kerry happens to be a lesbian and an African-American, yet neither of these aspects of her identity can answer the tough questions she faces. In Carol Anshaw's humorous "Mimosa," a sophisticated, successful lesbian observes with wry amusement her attraction to a selfish young woman named Kimberly. In both stories, the antagonists are intriguing young women adept at getting what they want in the urban world; whereas the protagonists worry more about ethics and appearances, these *doppelgangers* are wild, amoral outlaws. People who break the rules and appear to get away with it, at least for a time, are fascinating and often irresistible. Although we may distrust such people, we also envy their freedom and recognize our other selves in them.

In June Rachuy Brindel's "Service," a woman finds herself in a surrealistic gas station where self-service is apparently not an option and where everyone but her can get gas. A blizzard has obscured the landscape; in a world where no one seems to see her, does she even exist? The men in the garage advise her to wait for a boss named "Harve" who never comes. A writer known for her feminist retellings of classic myths, Brindel here evokes the eerie indifference of Beckett's *Waiting for Godot.*

Sara Paretsky's "The Man Who Loved Life" examines the psyche and character of Simon Peter Dresser, a man who would deny women their autonomy, their control of their bodies and selves. Like the hostile male environment encountered by the woman in "Service," Dresser's psychic landscape is unpleasant but compelling. Although he may be unable to understand himself, it is important for women to understand him and others like him. The discrepancy between Dresser's self-image as he is being praised in a speech and the actual Dresser—possessed by fear, anger, and hostility—is disturbing. Simon is his father's son, and he treats women accordingly. His daughter, however, may chart a new direction.

Mothers and daughters figure prominently in many of these stories, and S. L. Wisenberg addresses this

bond directly in "My Mother's War," wherein a
daughter must come to terms with the legacy of her
talented, eccentric mother and the Holocaust that was
her obsession. The mirrors and magic metaphors that
have been recurring throughout these stories are re-
solved here into the metaphor of art. The mother's
everyday ineptitude coexists with an artistic genius
and an overpowering predilection for sorrow. The
daughter must now assess her mother's life and her
own. Her mother's final artistic work is an artist's
conception of the Holocaust, not the thing itself. "So
there will be no cattlecars. No stench. My mother
made her Hell antiseptic." The story is a meditation
on the self and the world, on microcosm and macro-
cosm. Can one live with the weight of the Holocaust
as a personal and political legacy, whether or not one
wears the tattoo? Can one be an artist and reject the
aesthetic of suffering? Can one choose happiness?

Sandra Jackson-Opoku's "To Those Who Come
Behind Me" also explores the inescapability of the
past and the need to examine one's roots. Like Jackson's "The Island of the Rooster," this story takes
place in another country. And, as in the earlier story,
pregnancy plays a significant part. The narrator,
Mae, leaves a very possessive man and finds a man,
independent himself, who loves her and values her
independence. And in Africa, she finds that the other
is the self. Just as African countries have shaken off
colonialism, so has she. At one point her lover asks,
"Why are you here in Africa? Looking for yourself
outside of yourself," to which Mae replies, "But
Africa isn't outside of me. . . . It is in me. And I am
in it. It is my genealogy."

The final story anchoring the collection is Sharon
Solwitz's masterpiece "The Country of Herself." This
story, too, takes place in a foreign country. An intense
Israeli woman runs off with her small son, leaving her

baffled American husband to worry in Baghdad while she rushes headlong into her own tragic and haunting confrontation with the ancient story of Abraham and Isaac. Dvora is both modern and timeless. Her passion is political and religious and also personal. She loves her country, her husband, and her son, and it is precisely because of her love that her anger is so keenly felt, so uncompromising. Her husband, like the daughter in Wisenberg's story, struggles to understand another's obsession. He must try to make meaning out of what seems meaningless. I have deliberately placed this story last because after reading it, you will not want to read anything else for a while. You will need to touch a loved one, to reassure yourself that you and yours are alive and well. You will be acutely aware of what the Nigerian writer Chinua Achebe has said is the writer's function: "to afflict the comfortable and to comfort the afflicted." The best literature awakens us and sends us back into our lives, where we all must live our own stories.

Karen Lee Osborne

The Island of the Rooster

Angela R. Jackson

The hotel was a small one, pulled back from the street a little, as if it were aghast at the sights: the dirty water that hugged the curb after the short, intense rains; the beggars with dirty hands; the hawkers hawking cheap wooden masterpieces; the secret police with the magical ability to melt into landscapes. Behind us were the terraces of another place. I could see faces and splices of naked bodies through the palm trees. In the morning, I would sit on the balcony of my hotel room and listen for the crow of a rooster. I could never find him, although I turned in every direction.

The young woman who cleaned my room stood behind me on the balcony one morning. A stack of clean blue towels was cradled in her arms. She was slim-limbed, nineteenish, with white, white teeth and rich brown skin. Her eyes were boat-shaped. They shone when she talked about her baby daughter. Mariette talked about her daughter often. Mariette

told me, too, the story of the invisible rooster. Some of
the story. The rooster belonged to a rich American
friend of the island's President-in-perpetuity. The
American's villa was in the mountains, but his town-
house was behind our hotel. It was hidden behind a
high wall (except for the high windows and terraces
where flashes of flesh streaked by to disappear behind
palm leaves), and the rooster crowed from inside the
yard. The rich American was fattening the rooster,
Mariette told me. I asked her why. She stroked the
towels, shrugged her shoulders and turned away.

She continued with the stories of her tiny daughter.
She had recognized the baby-hunger in my eyes, had
recognized that I was a mother without child. She was
kind, and offered me stories of her daughter's
escapades. Regine was the little girl's name. Mariette's
eyes had shone in recognition that second morning
on the island when I'd found her on her knees scrub-
bing my bathtub. I'd told her my name: Regina Fields.
Regina Caeli. She'd smiled at me, leaned back on
her heels, and begun telling me about Regine.

This was our routine for the fortnight of my stay. I
would be up and out of my bed or Will's down the
hall, sitting on my balcony, bed or vanity bench. I
would hum and do beautifying things to my body,
things I rarely did at home. In the last cool of the
morning Mariette cleaned my room and talked to me.
By the time she finished her tasks and our talk, the
heat would have come and the timeless rooster would
be crowing crazily.

On hot days in the home of my girlhood, my
brother Nicodemus and I knelt on the couch before
the window with the fan in it. We'd look out onto the
street, the fast, whirring blades splicing our vision as

we watched the huge, mansion-like house across the street where the last white people lived. We watched the ashy-faced junkman harnessed to his refuse cart pulling up the avenue. And the vaseline-shiny girls jumping double Dutch, or double Irish in case of a tie, in front of our house. I remember the junkman humming and the jumping girls counting and Demus and me belting out a Sam Cooke song onto the street that held everything and the wind that carried everything away. When I watch fans spinning away moments, I remember those days when we knew everything and nothing could hurt us.

The fan twirled silently on the ceiling of the openair restaurant. Equally silent were the waiters who glided by in white Eisenhower jackets, flat-handed, carrying plates of shrimp and rice high, near their shoulders. If they had walked so heavily that the fan trembled on its axis, I would not have noticed them then any more than I did. I was leaning over a glass of white wine, gazing into Will's wonderful face. I traced the wide rim of the wine glass, and wished with the bindings of all my muscles and bones to trace instead the dark rims of Will's full lips.

There I sat, a brown woman soft with curves, face alive with moon-eyes shining up at the earth of his face. It was seven-fifteen and the sun had set while the wild rooster crowed behind his wall, the sound swelling and receding with the pacings I couldn't see but knew I did see.

"Somebody ought to put that bird out of his misery," Will peered past me into the night the hotel lights could not pierce. He squinted in murderous curiosity. "Why do they keep it?"

"Mariette says the rooster's fat and happy." I lifted my wine glass to shield some part of me from the annoyance that would come next.

"That's why he crows his stupid head off any time of day?"

"The owner's eccentric. Like owner, like rooster." I shrugged wanly, as though it was all my fault.

"Like a goddamned nuisance." Will pushed his plate away, fed up with everything: the island, the heat, the smell and taste of charcoal in every meal, the rooster, the conversation, me.

He had invited me to dine with him. He had invited me to come to the island; while he did his research, I could do mine. I'd said yes and registered into a room down the hall from him. Everything with Will was intense and abruptly closed. He tossed away cigarettes half-smoked. Before the song entirely ended, he broke the embrace and headed for the seats, pulling me from the pleasure of the music. Me? I made each song last a lifetime. The smoke of every one of his cigarettes hung in my eyes for hours after.

He lit a cigarette. I watched the thin signature rise on the lingering heat to meet the current sent down by the spin of the ceiling fan. I watched the smoke break up and float above our heads. I watched the fan and knew I dare not open my mouth like some girl who is safe beside her brother and knew I dare not sing up into a fan for the sheer mesmeric beauty of doing so. I could not afford to give away my own voice, amputated, then amplified by the force of the fan's so-swift-they-were-invisible blades. Sitting across the table from Will's disgruntled face, sitting inside my own helpless urge to soothe him, I knew I knew nothing and everything could hurt me. And that is why I had come to the island of magic, not only because Will had asked me. Magic offers proof of something—a body must levitate, holy feet must cross burning coals

and come out unscathed, a rabbit must be jerked out
by its ears from a black hat, a dove must float out of
scarves, a woman once sawed in two must be put
back together. I was ready to be faith-full and I
wanted a sign.

I did not know the name of the drum, but I had
heard that beat before, trapped and freed under my
own ribs. The rhythmic current of the drum shook the
room where I waited to consult with a priestess
of *vodun.** I had no idea if her knowledge were im-
promptu like a jackleg preacher's or earned, like an
earnest theologian's, through a large immersion in conversation with roughly transplanted African gods. The
room in which I sat questioning the credentials of the
spirit-physician was plain, with a dirt floor, clean as a
whistle that has blown through the teeth of the sleeping child. The child was sleeping on a cot in a corner
of the half-room that angled out like an elbow of the
room where I thought my suspicious thoughts. The
child, who was a girl in a worn, limp cotton slip-
dress, lay slanted across the sheeted bed. The sheet of
island-grown and woven cotton was delicious to lie
on, like the hotel sheets, but dingy from soapless
scraped-knuckle launderings. The girl sprawled loose

---

* *Vodun* (voodoo) is an African religion practiced by the mixed
African peoples of the Caribbean, especially Haiti. The word
vodun, according to R. J. Litz, is Dahomean for God or the
ultimate protective spirit. The supreme deity of the pantheon is
the Great Mother or Papa; the lesser deities are called *loa*, a
Congolese term meaning power. For further information, see Litz's
essay in *The Encyclopedic Dictionary of Religion*, edited by Paul
Kevin Meagher, Thomas C. O'Brien, and Sister Consuelo Maria
Aherne, SSJ (Washington, DC: Corpus Publications, 1979):
3693-3694. Alternate spellings of vodun are *voudou*, *vodou*, and
vodun.

and free in her sleep, like a ritual-dancer hanging in ecstasy. I imagined her dreams were in patois—a tongue dipped in the colors of colonial seventeenth century French, West African languages and scattered words of the original people of the mountainous soil. The musical patois paints vivid language colors over the barren land. An impressionistic rush of weeping and singing.

Once this island was ruled by Frenchmen who brought wigs and many kinds of wines, wives and courtesans, rules of court and slavery. I speak English, sit here in my Anglo-codified memory bank, just like the Americans who rule here now, using the President-for-life as a medium for life. A gofer for Coke, Kentucky Fried Chicken: the emptied bottles and cartons go sailing on the blue, bluer sea that surrounds the high ground and low slopes of the island.

The beggars, who wandered down from the hills, drawn by the lure of money and the lives it can buy, fled the eroding soil and its vanishing trees into the Port, capital city. They all know enough English. Enough to bludgeon me with, their misery battering at my eyes. One mother with a small child on her hip does not utter a word, but gestures to the child, through the body of the child whom she lifts like a shrug of the shoulder. The gesture is both question and plea. *What can you do about this starving child, American woman who is blacker than me?*

She shoves her dark palm in my face; the palm lines are obscured as if the hand itself were worn. I place an equally worn American dollar in her hand. It is an old game. And she nods her thanks and disappears with the big-eyed baby who haunts me.

This exchange occurred on one of the paths that curves around the presidential palace, a massive white colonial building, like a square of bones that sits impassively and opulently in the sun while beggars and the rest wander and stumble by.

The poorest of the Port lined up in front of the hotels—guides, beggars, hawkers waiting for women like me. Women they call American, because we bring American money. No matter that it is a small wad like gum that doesn't chew well, is dream money earned in tedium and monotony. Money for travel to an island known for its long-ago revolution, African revolution, and African religion, and government by an evil magic of disappearing acts. I had come in search of religion. Will had come in search of revolution. (We had come separately, renting separate rooms. But some nights we slept together, tumbling around the bed like two bad sleepers who cry out in their separate sleeps. What did anything mean?)

Outside the hotel, with a philosophy book in hand, leaning against a dark, prehistoric automobile was the young man who served as my guide this evening. He said that he was a university student and his uncle was a high priest of the vodun. He had knowledge of the religion that far exceeded the gaudy display of the Peristyle, where white-clothed dancers with blood-red scarves danced a flashy spectacle. Eating fire and turning their spines to writhing snakes in a neon den of Damballah devised for the voyeur appetites of Euro-tourists.

Through the intercession of the studious young man, I was waiting to consult with the real thing. A woman who, according to him, was not on the regular tourist route. Who did not offer her back to be ridden by the African gods for the benefit of shallow white Americans. Who served the people of the island, the occasional lucky Black visitor.

I had traveled down streets that twisted in the night like dark snakes. Walked between crowds of people massed under one roof, dancing to a drum that had

been beating since before forever, and would cease on
the morning after. It was a house party. The mood like
a basement set of my adolescence. I understood the
sweat and the sluggish, continuous energy of the jam.
People dancing alone or with partners bobbed up and
down like swimmers too content with the sun and sea
to stroke. I wasn't sure if that loud-smelling, humming
crowd was praying, practicing a ritual or simply getting down into a groove. I was frightened before I settled down into the home of it, before I inhaled deeply
enough to smell myself in the midst of the hot swaying and knee-bending, the shuffle across the floor, lan-
guid and superbly cool.

Bodies swelled around me; a sea of sweat swept me
along as I threaded through, behind my guide, on the
way to the room of the priestess. I lost my guide for a
time. I wandered in the music and the mood of the
crowd, which was oblivious to me or so inclusive no
one looked up from the ancient groove to welcome
me into it. They all understood that whoever was
there understood. They danced and I moved through
them, dancing and searching for my guide. I thought,
suddenly, as I peered over the shoulder of an undulat-
ing, toothless old man, I saw Mariette, my morning
confidante from the hotel, pushing through the dance.
She moved quickly, separate from the movement of
the gathering. Her eyes wild, her mouth open, she
disappeared.

She's in some trouble, I told the music in my head.
*She'll tell me tomorrow when I tell her about my mis-
sion here.* I wasn't satisfied with tomorrow, though; I
turned to trace Mariette's route through the room. But
she had vanished, and my guide had materialized. The
part of me that wanted to follow Mariette anyway I
silenced. *You have your own mission, Regina.*

I was ravenous to hear what the wise woman would
say about the question that simmered in me, made my

poor heart a boiling egg that was about to pop. It was a common pain: a not exactly unrequited love. I wanted more and more. I wanted a baby. My whole body ached with a full, roaring longing for a child. I was twenty-nine. My womb kept better time than the rooster. Every cell was talking genesis. "It's time. Increase and multiply." The noise of my hormones kept me awake nights. The ticking of clocks woke me from sound sleeps in my single bed. I'd call Will and tell him everything but what I really wanted. Will called me crazy.

I followed the guide.

She was an ordinary woman in a simple blue print dress. The fabric was man-made, not the cotton that grew on the island. A sweat film was on her earthy skin, a bronze sheen in her chemicalized hair, hair greased too heavily to hold the alien curl.

The female-priest sat in a little room. In that stifling room, shelves full of jars, bottles and statues, and boxes lined the walls. She gestured to me to sit. I sat primly, my knees pressed together tightly like old-fashioned Catholic birth control. She sat wide-legged like a man, her elbows on her knees. She drew symbols in the earth with a stick. I was ignorant of symbols. I forgot the presence of the guide who had brought me to her.

She took a big swallow from a dusty bottle halffull of a dark liquid. She gave me the bottle; I took a sip. A flicker of fire ran from my tongue to my throat and wound up in my chest.

She began to talk in the voice of a man. Her gestures took force and scope. She was talking in patois. The translator-guide told me what she said. He talked. I watched her mouth.

"You love this man. When he talks, he makes a garden of fire inside you. You love to see him stand up."

I nodded, dumbly amazed. I did like to see Will stand up. Other men looked like boys beside him. I thought of trees that brush sky. Trees that gathered storms inside them. How could she have known?

"You want a baby," the translator said she said. "A baby with this man. If this is meant to be, it will be. If it is not, she can help you. She will sacrifice a dove for you."

I looked at him.

"$200." He looked at me with a certain arrogance, as if he knew of my vast fortune.

"I don't have any money," I said sadly because I didn't and sadly because he wanted it.

"But in the States, you have money there." He was eager and anxious by then. Less demanding.

"Not really," I murmured. I saw myself counting pennies, hiding dollars, robbing Peter, promising to pay Paul.

He found a matchbook that he scribbled in with a Bic pen. "Here. This is the address. When you return to the States, you can send the money. She will make the sacrifice."

I nodded and looked around me. It was all heat and dust. Heat and dust. I edged my toe into the dirt floor. I was hot and tired.

The priestess who talked like a man sat with her elbows on her knees. Her polyester dress fell between her legs. Her child slept in a half-room. There was no running water. They spent half their lives on this island beating back the eroded dirt that flew down from the used mountains. They toted water from the sea.

Women in childbirth lay in and out of puddles of filthy water on the ground outside the tiny Port hospital.

The President-in-perpetuity married a mulatto heiress, and the nation was given a feast of balloons and cakes imported from France, flown in by jet. Bride and groom walked in white through the sanitized streets of the capital. Their white clothing threw back the sunlight. The smiling secret police threaded through the crowd and put heavy hands on grumbling onlookers. They silenced all protest. Men and women were dragged off to dungeons in the middle of the night. Their names were lost.

The smell and taste of charcoal was in everything, in our morning toast at the hotel, in the gravelly crow of the rooster I could not find. The last forests of the island fell for charcoal cooking. The bumpy land was left unprotected. Rain fell in tropical torrents and was washed into the omnipotent sea or lingered around the curbs of the capital.

I stared at the symbols the woman had scrawled into the soft earth.

The priest and her translator watched me. A wild play of despair must have crossed my face. I wasn't thinking of love and unborn babies. What about the born babies and their lives on this sad island? How sad they were, these two believers, selling God because he was all they had. I had only come to talk to spirits.

I wanted to say, "If I had the money, I'd send it so you could sacrifice a flock of doves to stop the hunger and misery here. Tell that to your goddamn gods!"

I said nothing but, "I'll try."

When I got back to the hotel, I told Will all about my visit to the priest. Even the parts I hadn't intended to divulge. He listened the way he does when he thinks the information is valuable: head cocked to one side, brow wrinkled, eyes fixed on the idea, head inching forward. I started to show him the matchbook with the address on it. I turned my purse inside out, dug through lipstick, blush, notebooks, first aid kit, coin purse, checkbook, but couldn't find the match-book.

"I lost it," I groaned, like a little girl who's lost her finger painting on the way home.

His comment was, "Serves you right for running to that circus shit. Niggers into that fetish foolishness and ain't got sense enough to wonder why they miserable. That fat, baby-faced fool in that big old mansion whipping magic shit on them just like his Papa did before him. Folks floating off this dying berg on broomsticks, instead of doing something serious about their lives. You thought these poor, pitiful people knew something about the power of God? Girl, grow up."

We were screaming at each other again. "You make me sick, William. You always looking down on somebody. I don't see you starting a revolution in America. I believe in the African gods. We don't use them. We got a mass failure of imagination. We can't see beyond . . ."

"Reality." He lit a cigarette.

"You act like Karl Marx slept with your mama."

"Don't start no signifying, Regina."

"Harpo, Chico, Groucho. One of them Marx boys."

"At least they were talking money. Not hawking some heaven in a filthy shack on an island I could pee across."

"And look at me," I said. "I'm running for help with *you*."

"I didn't put a knife to your throat, Li'l Regina. You gave it up freely."

"You dawg!" I slammed his hotel room door and regretted it. Then I opened it and slammed it again.

When I careened out of the hotel and tore into the dark streets, a young man approached me. His cheeks hugged the contours of his face, and his eyes were bright and burning behind dark glasses. He looked hungry and desperate. His shirt of a once fine material had seen better days, not on this island. He was flashy and sophisticated with soot on him.

"Miss, may I walk with you?"

"It's your country. But I want to be alone."

"You are like Greta Garbo. She was a star. She wanted to be alone."

He rambled in his pocket and pulled out a cigarette. He was a Marlboro man. He tilted it toward me, but I shook my head.

"What do you know about Greta Garbo?" I chided. Then I frowned because I heard the condescension in my tone and I did not like it. I was talking to a grown man.

"I want to be a star. In Hollywood. I will be a musician and an actor." He blew smoke in the dark air. I gave him a quick look. "You will be my sponsor? Will you help me enter the United States? Give me your address. I will give you mine. I will be a rock star."

"I can't help you," I told him gently.

We came to a street corner where a crowd congregated. A sermon washed the night air. The corner seemed brightly lit. People bumped into each other. Wobbly with religion. Across the way was a Kentucky Fried Chicken, closed.

"Do you know where Kentucky is?" I interrogated my companion.

He shrugged because he was angry and disappointed and disinterested. Then he perked up. "Is it near Hollywood?"

"Yes. They're both on Wall Street."

"I could climb this Wall Street. I could be a star with your assistance." He was ingratiating now. He even did me the favor of removing his sunglasses. We were at the ocean by then. It was endlessly black. It frightened me. And it fascinated me. The waves stirred. It was a big black body that shone back at

the moon. I lifted my camera and took picture after
picture. The flash popped and sizzled in the ripe plum
of night. Like quick bites.

The young man stood behind me, away from the
water. He smoked his cigarette and watched me watch
the ocean. It did not interest him. He had seen it before. Every day.

"It's wonderful," I enthused. I sounded to myself
like a tourist. But I knew I was in a minor religious
ecstasy. Blank sound welled up around me. It was the
ocean.

"In Hollywood I would be rich and famous," he
complained to the distant place where the black ocean
met the black and blue sky.

He was out of luck. And so was I. Will told me,
when I spoke to him again, that my pictures would
not turn out. I could not have the ocean.

I sat on the side of his bed, my heels turned in, camera on my lap. "If it wasn't for bad luck, I wouldn't
have no luck at all."

"I got a John the Conqueror Root," Will kissed at
me from across the room.

"Let me see," I said. I stood with my legs apart like
a gunslinger facing another gunslinger in the middle of
town. My skirt fell between my thighs when he
opened the sliding door to the balcony. He sent a
small breeze in my direction. He walked out into the
night with a drink in his hand.

I went after him and watched him leaning over the
railing, sipping his rum.

"The fellas in front say you got big juju," I told his
back.

"Shit. I know *that*. How much money they want to
tell me something I can use?"

"I didn't ask."

"I'm surprised. You fall for any superstitious sob
story. You the world's biggest sucker."

"I guess I am." I yielded to the obvious. After all, I was standing on the balcony of his hotel room, talking to his back. It was a beautiful back, long and wide, and slim at the hips. Mannish. Sometimes I hated it.

"I bet they got a signal they flash through the streets when you hit the outdoors. Here she come, the free-hearted woman. Everybody got you pegged."

"So what do you want from me?" I asked.

He looked at me then. His eyes were large like a boy's and full of fear that fluttered up and fell down again when he dropped his lids and lifted his drink and took a long swallow. I watched his throat work. I was aching.

"You may have a root, but you are a luckless man," I growled, and some of the ache went out of my throat and misted my eyes. I didn't believe what I said. I was the unlucky one. I was in love with him.

Will woke up, rolled over on his side and lifted the travel clock. It wasn't six yet. He rolled over and looked at me. Neither one of us said anything. He kissed my quiet mouth. He dipped down to catch my nipple in his teeth, like a long-necked bird breaking the still surface of the water to bring up a writhing fish. He opened me in one stroke like an expert swimmer, and I floated under him, breathlessly. The roar of sex so loud in my ears I couldn't hear that pampered rooster, but I knew he must have been crowing at the sunrise.

I listened to Will in the half-light. "I don't hate these people, Regina. They're me. How could I hate myself? I'm impatient with the circumstance. I can't stand this existence for anybody. People not supposed to suffer so. Fuck a god that lets 'em, cause it ain't a

god. It's a blind beggar standing on a corner asking
for prayers to rattle in his cup. And whoever worships
it is the blind leading the blind."

When I went back to my room, Mariette was sitting
on my bed, drying her eyes. She stood up quickly
when I came in.

"Sit down," I said. "Finish what you were doing."
She sat down again.

"I thought I saw you last night." I searched her face
for trouble.

The rooster crowed.

She began to cry.

She cried until I thought my heart would break. My
few hot tears over Will were venial, misdemeanor,
compared to her bent-back sobbing thrown up from
the womb, wrenched out of the heart. The force of
her weeping shook the obligatory scarf off her head.
Her serene dark face was torn up with crying. In one
moment the sound of the poor woman's weeping and
the rich man's rooster's crowing blended in a rude
ecstasy. The rooster finished, then she finished.

The smell of charcoal climbed through the window,
enveloped us like a seventeenth century courtesan.

Mariette put the towel to her face for the last time.
Then she looked at me through red, puffy, boat-
shaped eyes.

"Can I help you?" I could feel a fragment of my
soul offered over to her.

She blinked, smiled tremulously and shook her head.

"Is it Regine?" I asked. Her red eyes opened wider.
And panic opened in me.

I started to act like my mother when one of her
neighbors has an emergency. "I don't have much, but .
. ." Mama says as she searches in her pocketbook for
the last dollar or two. I reached for my purse, but she
put her hand over mine. Her hand was work-rough,
stern.

Her face was close to mine, held like a hand mirror image in front of me.

"No," said she who had seen everything I owned, my worn, pretty dresses, my lingerie, my one or two new pieces.

She gathered her towels and scrambled through the charcoal aroma out of the room, chattering about Regine all the while. Regine this. Regine that. Talking too fast and faster.

That afternoon Will and I toured outside the city. We followed a thin, rough road into the mountains. Leaning out the car window, I looked down a cliff, watched the wheels of our car hug the rim of the road. Will was whistling. I stared down into the valley of white blossoming fields.

"What's that blossoming down there?" I pointed with my sunglasses into the valley, but Will kept his eyes on the road.

"Cotton, baby," he answered, then went back to whistling "Frankie and Johnnie" à la Sam Cooke.

I looked at the path. We rode without speaking. His whistling segued into "You Send Me."

Figures rose from behind the curve in the road in front of us. Will slowed down; he whistled nothing that I knew. The figures approached, became particular. Every one of them was dressed in gray—four women and two men shadowing a gray casket carried by four more men who walked slowly but without straining. The casket was not large.

"Jesus Christ." I couldn't stop staring at the casket swaying gently in the mountain air. Will just whistled under his breath, a broken tune. And we were all part of a dance. Will slowed to a halt. The funeral procession passed us by on the narrow roadway, so close I could read the somber expressions of the men, the penetrating anguish of the women conveyed in the tight, lucid gestures of their interminable march.

One woman, thirtyish, exquisite with grief, her eyes charcoal encircled in red flame, her lips chapped and bitten raw. *The mother.* I ached between my legs. I could look only at her. When they finally passed us, I pulled in the ragged rope of my breath; the twisted cord hurt in my chest.

Will and I didn't talk for the rest of the ride. We pulled up at last in front of the castle turned factory. We drifted apart in the perfumery.

What had been a clumsy silence turned into a silent quarrel at the perfumery. I wandered absent-mindedly behind the guide who chanted the biography of a bottle of cologne, from vetiver to vanity table. A sour taste was in my mouth and I could not smile. Will lavished attention on a café au lait model named Jorgina; he sprayed her earlobes with sample scents that sparkled in glass containers on glass counters. The model giggled prettily into the glass, fogging it. The factory was a castle dating before the revolution. The edges of the stone turrets crumbled; cracks ran through the huge stones like lightning seams. But the structure held. Will's girl danced along like a ghost from the past.

The sun glared across the stone. I looked down into fields of green vetiver. I made conversation with the tour guide, feigning a deeper interest in the perfumery than I felt. Learning more than I wanted to know.

Will invited Jorgina to join us for a drink in the hotel restaurant.

✦ ✦ ✦

"They cut down the trees from the mountains to make two-by-fours they ship to France. But they don't

have wood for their own shacks. And not enough
trees to keep the ground under them from slipping
away." In the restaurant-bar Will sat with the wide-
eyed model here for a swimwear shoot. Aghast at the
poverty of the island, she opened her eyes wider still
to Will, as if turning to him for salvation.

"Why do these people behave so self-destructively?
Don't they have ecologists?" she implored.

Will snapped, "Money. Money's why," because he
can only talk to stupidity but so long. But it was just
long enough to make me jealous. I grew sadder, more
eager to tie us together. Maybe I could save $200 for
a sacrifice.

I dreamed we lay down together in a field of vetiver.
It scratched our skin, but we didn't notice as we fused
and tangled legs. Laughter and the smell of vetiver
were in my wide-open nostrils, in my throat.

I awakened to find the scent heavy in my hair.
Will said, "Your hair smells like the factory."
I said, "Kiss my —."
"It smells like perfume."
I smiled and told him to kneel down in the bathtub
so I could wash the sweat from his head. I told him
my dream. How sweet it was to lie down in the per-
fumed fields.

He just said, "You not the first randy American
romantic who wanted to get laid in a bed of vetiver."

Soapy water ran in his eyes, and he howled so
loudly I laughed. But my laugh was hollow as his
howl. I was disappointed in his response. It had been
a beautiful dream. Roughly, I slapped the soap from
Will's eyes. I rinsed and wrapped his coarse hair and
led him like a blindman into the room.

The breeze from the open balcony door was thick
with charcoal. It swept the vetiver from my hair, until
only a trace remained. Naked, I sat down in the chair
that faced the floor-length mirror. Naked, Will sat on
the floor between my thighs. I began to part his rough-
soft hair. I oiled his scalp with an oil I had bought at
the perfumery.

"What's that you putting on my head?" he growled
languidly, too content with my pampering to offer
rebuke.

"Vetiver oil."

"You think all your dreams must come true, don't
you, girl?"

He looked at me in the mirror without blinking.
His arms anchored my thighs. His back to my geni-
tals, in the mirror his chest was a shield before my lap.

Four levels of nakedness. Music sounded in the
bright circle of time, endless and ethereal. The two of
us resting in an endless dance.

I had washed his mustache and beard until the gray
strands shimmered with life. I touched the oil to the
gray, and it turned silver. I felt like an alchemist. He
was magic. The silver. I knew then the years between
us and the stories he knew that I did not.

I told him about Mariette, her tears. He told me
what the busboys told him about the rooster, what
Mariette would not tell me.

The owner of the rooster suffered from a wasting
disease. Leukemic but not leukemic. Pneumonic but
not pneumonic. Venereal but not venereal. For all his
wealth, he had found no solution outside the realm
of religion. He waited under the to-and-fro flow of
servant-held fans on his veranda for God to cure or
kill him. He sweated, sipped bottled water and turned

his full attention to a pet rooster. (His American
friends who dined with him at the palace of the
President-in-perpetuity took his preoccupation with
the rooster as a sign of soft-hearted eccentricity. Such
devotion to an animal coupled with disdain for
humans was not unusual to lovers of pedigreed
poodles and Chihuahuas, owners of chestnuts and
sleek, heaving blacks that broke racing records. The
President-for-life, inbred, half-caste, tuxedoed, gazed
at his failing, rooster-doting friend with knowing, half-
closed eyes.) The sick, rich American fattened the
scrawny island rooster, feeding it perfect kernels of
corn, charcoal-scented toast, imported apples, figs,
pomegranates and hearts of palm from the palm of his
right hand. The rooster's coat turned lustrous and its
body grew plump. It grew lunatic with prosperity and
crowed throughout the day.

Early the next morning, there was running under
my balcony. First one pair of shoes pounding the
terraces below, then five, then twenty. I ran to the win-
dow-door. Hotel employees, stunning whites on their
rich skin, shouted in each other's faces. They
gesticulated with abandon. I couldn't understand a
word of it. I stepped onto the balcony. Will was on
his. We had gone our separate ways in the night.
    "What's happening?" I shouted across the railing
at Will.
    "Did you hear that goddamned rooster this morn-
ing?" he yawned, leaning over the rail languorously.
He wore linen pajama bottoms which looped down so
I could see the cut in his buttocks. He wasn't listening
for my answer. I hadn't heard anything. I hadn't heard
his phone call asking me to come to bed with him.
Hair shining, beard sparkling, he'd dressed and gone

out. He spoke the language of the people. He moved freely on the island. The tall American. The Black juju-man from the States.

He spoke the language. "Somebody stole that rich faggot's bird."

"How do you know?"

"I'm listening to the busmen right now. They know. They're talking about the sick Yankee fag with the fat rooster somebody kidnapped. They're talking about how mad the President's gonna be."

The talk of the crowd diminished. The cooks had gone back to their stoves. The charcoal woman got ready for breakfast. Pieces of the land's last forests were fed to the hotel fire.

Will patted his taut stomach. "Somebody ate that fat bird." He was gleefully certain of the fate of the bird.

The hubbub below dispersed into triumphant laughter as the workers went back to their posts. I watched their return to the status quo. Then I looked at the high wall that could not hold the rooster after all.

"There are other kinds of hunger, Will." I talked across balconies the way I talked across bed.

"Woman, don't start. It's too early in the goddamn morning." He hitched up his bottoms, pinched in his mouth.

"I wasn't talking about *us*."

"It's all about us." He looked through me for the longest time. He must have seen my heart beat, my baby-longing, my soul-piece I had handed the weeping Mariette, and what I had given him. He must have seen my self straining out of me. His gaze softened, and his voice, when he asked me if I would go with him on the glass-bottomed boat to the coral reef.

✦ ✦ ✦

I was looking at the ocean floor, dreaming of a
rooster crowing. The bottom of the boat was cut
out, then filled with glass. Tourists, mostly French
businessmen with their wives or mistresses, sat on
narrow, wooden benches and gazed into the water at
the coral formations and the bright, little fishes.

"Amazing," I whistled down into the glass.

"It's like an interrogation room," Will breathed into
my ear so the Europeans would not hear. Will stopped
talking to white people around April 4, 1968. He only
engaged in rudimentary dialogue with them. "You
know," he said, "the police see in and the prisoner
can't see out."

"Do they have inquisition rooms on this island?"
I stared out at the blue shades of sea, signifying
changes in depth, and the hushed sun that was hot
on my body in the orange sundress.

"I hope I never know. Whoever stole that rich
Yankee's rooster is gonna die in a dirty little room."

A gold and green fish scuttled under us. The heavy
salt air was strangely hard for me to breathe.

The lean, ochre guide told us to line up to walk
into the ocean. I slipped out of my sundress. The sunlight dazzled on the fuchsia surface of my swimsuit.
Will was all beautiful black, the color of strong coffee.
He walked in front of me. I watched the sway of his
buttocks in purplish-black trunks. He slid into the
ocean, took goggles from the guide and stuck his
bearded face into the blue water.

Faithful to the ease of his entry, I walked into the
water, stepped like Peter behind Christ onto the heavy
sea. The coldness of the water woke me from the
trance of sexual hypnosis. I broke trust with Will and
panicked at the awesome weight of the ocean. Brine-
water swayed and shot into my mouth. My eyes
turned to stone.

"I want to get back in the boat." My stunned whisper drifted toward the guide. I had lost my feet in the
water. My arms rode the sea away from me. My voice
began to rise. I could feel Will's eyes on me.

"I want to get back in the boat." The sea came
alive, opened to swallow me. Will snatched my hand.
He snapped at the guide in the language I couldn't
understand.

"Stand up, Regina." Will had my elbows. I unlocked my legs and stood on the ocean floor. "Now
you feel like a fool. Get back in the goddamn boat."

I didn't care that the water was only as high as my
chin. I didn't care that I was a fool in fuchsia, drip-
ping salt and water as I climbed back into the tourist
boat.

Will, his face in the water, floated on the surface of
the shallow reef. I sat like a happy convalescent on the
narrow bench and watched the bodies, like dead men
and women, lying on top of the blue water. Coral divers with rotting, broken teeth clucked at me, then
gracefully curved out of the boat to hunt for loose
coral and conch shells. They circled the still corpses of
the tourists. I watched Will play dead for a time, then
roll over and swim away beyond the arc the divers
made. The wind swept by as I leaned over the edge of
the boat and looked forlornly toward shore.

The priestess in the dusty room, Mariette crying
into the newly laundered towel, the child sleeping
through drumbeats, the translator with desperate eyes,
the aspiring media star in search of a patron angel,
the broken-toothed beggars persistent with
hunger—images rose in me until I could have crowed
with despair, swelled in my eyes and brimmed over,
splashed down my cheeks. Shocked and embarrassed
by my sudden tears, I put my head in my lap and
rubbed my eyes raw with my sundress.

A diver, salt settled like ash on his shoulders, lifted himself into the boat. He stood in front of me, blocking the sun, his bony knees torn and bleeding from the keen edges of the coral. I did not look at his face, but reached instinctively for my purse and the first aid kit in it. I took out the tiny tube of antiseptic cream, then tilted my face to look at him. He would not take the medicine I offered him. Instead he handed me a large conch shell full of sea-smells, and quoted me a price. I gave him all the money I had in my purse. He shook his head at me, and gave me a dollar change. Then he sat on the floor of the boat and wrapped dirty rags around his bleeding knees.

Suddenly, Will splashed out of the water and splashed down next to me. He grabbed the shell and turned it over in his wet hands. He put the shell in his lap, on top of his penis, then he put his wet arm around my shoulder.

"Fill this thing with tar, let a charcoal ember burn on it for one minute, sprinkle Ambergris on the charcoal and pray like crazy for the thing you have to have. The next Friday at 3:00 a.m., pick violet leaves and call on three good loas. Put all of this under your pillow and go to sleep and dream things. When you wake in the morning, write down your dream and don't tell anybody about it, not even me, or it won't come true." He tilted my face toward his. He looked at my red eyes. I could see the salt in his beard, making it grayer than it was.

"How do you know?" I asked his mouth.

He kissed me tenderly on my eyes.

I inhaled the smell of him and the ocean; they were the same. We were locked in the sweetest embrace, as if we had turned to the most delicate coral. He breathed into my ear. Time held us in the circles of its fingerprints. The painful pictures were dissolving in me. Then he shifted his torso, chuckled and clucked like a chicken in my ear.

"I thought you loved the ocean, girl. Scared the shit out of you. You tourists." He moved away from me, made an arc with his arm that included me with the wives, mistresses, and businessmen. He tossed me the conch shell, reached for the antiseptic tube and dabbed medicine onto the scrapes on his knees. I wanted to break his neck with one stroke, the way a vodun-priestess kills a pigeon, a dove, or a rooster for sacrifice. But I laughed, instead, at the irrational fear that had made me come out of the ocean and into the boat.

On the ride back to shore, Will slept with his head in my lap. I stroked the tight, salt-gritty curls on his head and thought of how Mariette's eyes would shine when I gave her the conch shell.

The translator-guide of the vodun-priestess was standing outside the hotel when Will and I walked up, hand in hand.

He sidled up to me. "You left this, mademoiselle." He handed me the matchbook with the loa-woman's name and address printed on it. He grinned at Will, looking him up and down. He made a big production of noting how tall Will was, leaning way back like he was looking for the top of a skyscraper. He stuck out his chest. "Was good consultation, was it not?" He looked at me as if he personally had answered my prayers. "She is the most powerful priestess on the island. Yes?"

Will had walked away from us. He stood at the entrance to the hotel.

I noticed then the peculiar quiet of the square. The ubiquitous beggars were not there. The presidential palace was somehow larger, whiter.

The translator looked into my eyes and continued a conversation I didn't know had ever begun. "The maid's child is fine. *She* has made a sacrifice."

The last light in the late afternoon disappeared into his grin. And charcoal smoke thickened the air. I backed away from the smiling translator and ran to Will, who stood impatiently waiting for me. Will scooped me up; he put his arm around my waist, and we walked together like wounded allies into the quiet lobby.

As we skirted the open-air restaurant, the fan was motionless, but the air had picked up speed and cooled. Busmen gazed at us out of red eyes. Then they came together and whispered; their shoulders held tight with tension as they balanced plates of the sea-food specialty.

"I wouldn't eat here tonight." Will talked very low, so that the sound of his voice curved only toward me.

I thought the only danger would be too much salt leaked onto the heaping plates. Someone, a woman, was weeping, but I could not see her. I knew it. But maybe it was the wind that came with the dark. It had not seemed so sudden or portentous when I had gazed at the guide and watched the afternoon's light vanish into his grinning mouth.

The rain shook loose from anchors in the sky. We ran through it, Will and I. Across the patio and up the stairs to our rooms, we ran and ran.

The maid's cleaning cart stood in front of my closed door. We shot into the room, our clothes and dregs of the sea clinging to us as we moved noisily, strangely drowsily and keenly alert. Will searched the closets and the bath.

A pile of towels lay at the foot of the bed.

"Mariette?"

I went to the balcony. There was only rain.

"Where have they taken her?"

Will didn't answer.

I pulled the towels to my sopping chest, and a brown, star-like thing fell out.

"What's that?" Will said, as if he already knew.

I picked it up but didn't answer him.

"Put it someplace." He looked at me, his eyes full of apprehension.

I shoved the once living thing into my wet bra, and then I started shaking and could not stop. Death poised next to my heart. I kept it under my clothes until I left the island three days later. I do not remember with clarity the last three days. Will went outside the hotel, mingled with the guides and hawkers. He brought back the story of Mariette and Regine, who would have died.

"Where is she?" I asked him.

"The little girl is in the mountains."

"Mariette?"

He wouldn't say.

I have the dirty matchbook with the loa-woman's address. I never used it. I have the conch shell, but I did not follow Will's ritual. I have the rooster's claw that scratched my breast where I hid it. These things are in a drawer under well-worn lingerie and pouches of magic powder and vetiver.

I know a motherless child breathes in her lonely sleep on the island while a sickly, rich white man feeds a new white rooster for his pleasure and his cure. I am a childless woman who has soothed the hunger inside herself with other hungers, more terrible, more tenuous. I pray for an island and beyond it, for an ocean of beggars and more than them or me.

Months later, I wake in the middle of the night. The smell of charcoal is so thick I think I will smother. The ocean crests into my mouth, and I think I will drown. The rooster crows and crows, and Will shakes me and tells me to wake up, Regina, wake up, when I thought I was awake.

"Who's crying?"

I sit up, disoriented, in the arc of Will's arm. I look around the dark room in every direction, but I cannot find the rooster crowing behind the wall. I cannot find the woman weeping until Will whispers, "It's you, Regina. It's you."

The Foreigner in the Blood

Mary Gray Hughes

The daughter of Leon Esteban, yes *the* Leon Esteban, committed him to a private sanatorium for elderly incompetents in July. She, Clara Rasmussen, for that was the name of the man she had married and was the name she used even professionally, signed the committing forms as a member of his family and his potential guardian, and two other doctors signed the psychiatric reports required by the law, a model law, too, which Esteban himself had drawn up for the state years ago. It was all done "according to Esteban," as his colleagues used to joke. And indeed the precipitating incident, the immediate cause of his committal, made a case as classic as any of those in his textbooks.

"Who is that strange man in my house?" he had said over the phone to his secretary and assistant. "I tell you there is a stranger in the house," and the *s*'s of his speech hissed heavily, as they did more and more the last few years. The secretary at once asked

what he meant and what was he talking about, and as
she began asking questions it seemed there was only
some misunderstanding or other, and he said it was all
quite all right and that he was on his way up to bed.
She told him he had been working too hard, which
was true. Two nights later he called her again, waking
her from a deep sleep. "I tell you there is a strange
man in my house. Who is he? What is he doing
here?" By the time she was awake enough to begin
talking to him and questioning him, the matter
seemed again of no importance. Some shadows he had
seen. In the morning she did not mention it, and neither did he. It was not until the third time he called
her, in the afternoon this time, crying out, "Who is
this man? I am afraid, understand? Afraid. There is a
strange man here in the hall beside me," that she remembered the phone was in front of the large hall mirror, and that it was himself he saw.

She had gone at once to his home, and she had
stayed with him, without protest from him either, until
Clara could cancel her appointments and get a plane
out from New York.

Esteban's doctor agreed Esteban must have more
care now than in the past. A little more care in circumstances somewhat different, somewhat more careful of
him, and he could continue his life much as before. It
was decided he would be best off in some good private home. He could continue his work there and
everything would be made easier for him. Many arrangements had to be made, and both women were
enormously busy. Any number of homes and special
hospitals for the old or sick had to be investigated and
one selected. Esteban's books, papers, and notebooks
had to be sorted, since he could not take them all with
him. And there were the legal papers. They worked
night after night to get it all done. Esteban worked
with them, and seemed tactfully grateful for their help.

He said so, sometimes. Then again, he would be quite different.

"You enjoy it too much," he said to them. "You, you women. Interviewing hospitals. Signing papers. You love it."

"Now, now, you know you don't mean that," his secretary said, not so much as lifting her head from the drawer where she was going through notes of his early cases and throwing out duplicates. But Clara Rasmussen looked hard at him, her father, this clever man. How much in fact was he failing? How much of that was the querulousness of age, and how much was sheer malice, the irresistible dig? He'd always loved to tease her by making fun of her seriousness, her conscientiousness, her hard work. It was only by this she had got ahead. She hadn't his brilliance. She knew she was a drudge, but she was competent. She had published. Little Earnesta, he called her. He had done it pleasantly enough, but she had winced. How much of what he said now was intended? Did he really think she enjoyed committing him? As she stared at him, his long dark face split open like an apple with a white grin.

"Well, little Clahra," he said, for so the name came out on his foreign tongue. "Well? You were always the one who liked measurements, no? Have you decided? Am I 100 percent certifiable? Or 99 percent? Or maybe . . . 63 percent?"

"Papa, stop it. Tell me which of these books you want to take. Pick out which ones you want. If you change your mind, I can always bring you different ones later."

"Later? What do you mean later? How long are you staying?" So hopefully, so anxiously and hopefully, completely different from his manner the second before.

On the spur of the moment, because of his face, she said, "All summer. Peter can come out and spend his vacation here, and I'll stay here all summer."

And Esteban spun away from her and half-ran out of the room.

"He's so up and down, so all mixed up," Clara said to the secretary.

"Now, now, never mind. He's old, you know, Clara," the secretary answered.

When the time came Clara drove Esteban to the Home in his car, which was piled with books and files and, in suitcases and on hangers, quantities of Esteban's lovely clothes. He was to have a corner room. Clara had seen to that. And she had replaced the dark green, flowered curtains with plain good white ones. She had not been able to get them to repaint the light green walls.

From a few steps into the center of the room Esteban stood surveying it. In his linen suit, among the institutional furniture, surrounded by short-sleeved attendants bringing in his belongings, he was completely out of place.

"Well, do you like it? Is it all right, do you think? Papa?" Master, she might have called him. Teacher. A giant in the field. He had known Freud. He would certainly see the farce in it, that he should be here, in the little corner room with good curtains at the two windows (special rate for two windows) and not enough bookshelf room to hold even the books that he, Esteban himself, had written.

"I couldn't get them to paint the walls yet," Clara said. "But I could have a painter come in and do it. I'm sure of that."

"You can't change everything. See, am I not being good?"

"Papa, stop that. Stop. If you don't like it, I'll take you right out. You know that. We can make other arrangements. . . . oh yes we can, don't look like that. You could stay at home, if you want. I could shift my practice here."

"And Peter? Nonsense, Clahra. No such thing. Some things now I must give up. It must be. Let strangers deprive me of things, that is better than your doing it. Now, send Alice soon to help me with the typing. And you must again be my assistant until I am settled. It will be fine, yes? Only, you are sure they understand about all this, and you and Alice are to come and go as we please? Good. One thing, tell that little man, the fat one, what's his name?"

"Hoffman."

"Tell him to stay away from me. I don't like that little fat man."

"But he's the director," she said. "He's not really fat. He's quite good. Really. He told me they were honored to have you here. He knows your work."

"Ha ha ha. Honored, fine. Honored. I know that type. He's my jailer, Clahra. Only I don't have to like him. Remember? All the best analysts say that. I don't have to like anyone for such a thing."

It turned out to be unfortunate about the director's name. Esteban said he could never remember it, or never remember it correctly. He delighted in making variations on it: Hausmann, Hausfrau, Hauptman, Helpman. Even Faust. But occasionally he was genuinely not able to remember the name, and his sharp bright face would bunch up with the effort, as if something were jammed, and in an instant he would grow old, ancient, before one's eyes. Yet other than this, he accepted it remarkably well, Clara thought. He worked long hours in his corner room, dictating from his old notes and correcting the drafts of typescripts.

He called for one volume after another to check references or reread papers. The finished papers piled up on his desk with Clara working hard as his assistant, as she had years ago, but with a great difference now. She had her own career and her own life, which had to be kept up as well.

She established her family in Esteban's home and took over the few patients he still had. She commuted by jet to New York each week to take care of her own practice. She had never had such a busy, expensive life of such sophistication. She loved the jets and all the rituals of flying: the care, the cocktails, even the food. She had never felt so solemnly adult, so important. And everywhere people in her profession knew of her father's trouble and how she was manag- ing it. Everyone asked about him, and as in her early days as a practicing analyst she had amused psychia- trists with stories of the great Esteban's problems with American pronunciation, or American slang, now she told over and over the classic story of how he had not recognized himself in the mirror, and so had been committed. It was a remarkable story. Whenever she told it there would be a pause of silence afterward. Then she would be asked how he was doing, and she would tell of his fights with Hope-man. It went over very well. Too well. She found it hard to stop. One rainy wretched day she realized she had twice, in different groups at a New York cocktail party, brought the conversation around so that she could tell her story on Esteban. And that's what it had become—a story on Esteban.

"Enjoying it too much?" Esteban had said. Was she? Probably. Yes, probably, damn him. He knew. Hadn't he written, in a famous paper, *If only the young would take as their revenge the damage time will inflict upon their parents, they would not need to indulge in those actions or thoughts which sully their minds with guilt.* The word "sully" had been particularly admired in analytic circles. When Clara first read the paper (she was the most talented of his protégés at this time, and his "closest critic," it amused him to say) she said only, assuming as she often did the right to a much greater understanding of the United States than he, a foreigner, could have, "Papa, you never will understand Americans must do something themselves. They don't get satisfaction from anything that just happens. They are first and always doers."

He had laughed. So many American words, like "doer," amused him. But he had not changed anything in the paper. Sometimes he made changes when she had suggestions, most often he did not. And everything he did was successful anyway. Everyone admired him.

Except at the Home. At the Home, Esteban was beginning to have difficulties. When she visited him and found him working, as she always did, and worked with him, he seemed as active and agile, as excited about his work and as alert, or almost as alert, as ever. It seemed then only because of some matter of strange convenience that he should be living in a tiny corner room in a home for the senile and deranged. Yet the staff told her other things: that he could never remember how to get to the dining hall and an attendant had to be sent for him. That he didn't want to change out of his clothes at night and get into his pajamas. That he threw things on the floor. Petty little things. Institutional offenses. Half deliberate, she suspected, done with the malice of the angry but sane. He had always liked jokes. If these were stranger ones, pettier ones, who could blame him? All the silly rules of the place, all the dull people staffing it. He was bound to hit back. *She* had no trouble with him.

Yet one of their complaints about him, she could see, did give them real trouble. That was his dislike

for the director. It was amusing to call Hoffman
names behind his back, but lately Esteban had begun
doing it openly, and often before other patients. It dis-
turbed them, the director said. "Half-man," Esteban
yelled at him, right in the common living room. And
when Hoffman went on by, Esteban had spat after
him onto the floor. It was foolish, childish, Clara told
Esteban. He didn't need to do that sort of thing. He
could avoid Hoffman if he wished.

"Don't worry," Esteban said. "You always worry
too much. Bring me some oranges, Clahra. We never
get any decent fruit in this place. Bring me some Spanish oranges I can suck on," and he held his hand up
before his face with the fingers curved around an
imaginary orange, "something I can get some juice out
of."

Blood oranges, he meant. She bought a net sack of
them at the market south of town.

"What a gloomy name for an orange," her husband said. "Who wants to eat blood? It's that old
macabre Latin sense."

"He's not Latin. He's Spanish," Clara said, but she
wasn't paying much attention. She was packing food
in a small kit. Her husband watched with a bland
weighing eye and from time to time would reach in
and rearrange a box or the thermos so that it would
fit compactly. He was much better at this sort of thing
than she was. He often came along, chatting with her
and helping when she tidied the house or put away
the clothes because he was the better at it and because
it was a pleasant time to talk. He was a geologist who
ran a small firm that did consulting for oil companies.
He knew nothing of analysis. Her work was always
an amazement to him, as was his to her, and they constantly brought each other gifts of novel information
and delighting, fresh ideas, for their minds, like most
of the hours of their days, ran along quite separately

but side by side, with hundreds of ties across. Her father, however, was not one of them and, with Esteban, Rasmussen shared nothing.

"I'm taking him out for a drive," she said. "I hate seeing him cooped up in that place all the time. It must get on him. It gets on me. All those dreadful people, sick and old or addled. And the dimwitted staff. I can't work with him there anymore." She could not focus on him, she meant. She felt she could not seem to see him, could not get through to him to do any real work, anything that was not the simplest routine.

"Well, be careful."

"Don't be silly, he's my father," she said.

Esteban was not expecting her. He was standing by one of the two windows. He was without jacket and tie, and he was leaning forward with his hand touching the screen. It was a heavy one of the sort that could not be opened from the inside. She was sure it had not been there when she had taken the room.

"Papa," she said. He seemed disconcerted by her being there. "I came early," she said. "It's Sunday . . . and I'm quite early."

"Yes. All right. I was thinking. I have been thinking of the meanings of the disrobing of Christ."

"Good heavens."

"Have you thought about it? Think about it."

"Okay, if I have to. But later. I've got a surprise."

He brightened. "Oh, listen, Clahra, I have a surprise. I, too. Such a funny thing this morning. Let me tell you. It's really very funny. Hoffman came to see me. He came in," and he began to mimic Hoffman, for despite his accent and his sharp Spanish face, he had a gift for mimicry and could catch the voice and look of his victim. "'Ah, ah, ah now, good morning

now, ah now, Dr. Esteban.' He's never learned I am
not an M.D. We weren't in those days," he said. Then
he switched roles again, drooping his shoulders and
pushing out a nonexistent tummy. "'My dear Dr. Esteban, I wonder if, ah now, you couldn't help me out.'
You see the direction, Clahra? I am to help the big director. Oh I am to be flattered." She began to smile.
What a fool Hoffman was to think he could try anything like that with Papa. "So I, I keep a straight still
face, very still . . . like in a session, understand? 'I'm
in need of some references for a paper,' he says. 'I've
been doing a little, ah now, ah now, work, ha ha.' He
can't even come out and say the word decently. He
doesn't know the meaning of the word and knows it,
so he gives a little apologetic laugh, 'ha ha,' when he
says 'work.' 'I've been doing a little work, ha ha,' he
says, 'with chlorpromazine among our more, um, ah
now, elderly patients here.' All the time I am blank, a
blank face, but just beginning to let it go a little stupid, a little slack and stupid. Not too much. 'My assistant seems to remember some work along these lines
done in a veterans' hospital. We thought perhaps you,
ah now, perhaps you might remember. . . .' He had
even set me such a simple task, you see, so I could
give the answer and get the prize. That paper by Belan-
jian and Emerson. Oh just the right degree of difficulty. But recent, to test how much I remembered
recently."

"Oh Papa, really you can't be sure of that!" But she
could not help laughing too. He was impossible, her
father.

"On he goes," Esteban said, "giving me all the
clues, more and more, suggesting a name, even their
names, and I get a bit stupider, a bit slacker. He calls
the names out, and I stare. And oh he is happy. He begins to smile. I am foolish, he thinks. I am foolish and
he is quite sure. He smiles, you see, he thinks he

knows just how the mind is gone. He is happy, he is certain. He is ready to go. I let him take a step, another, then I straighten my face, stern, stern, the look of a father to an errant son, indignation, the hard stare, and I say, in good medical Latin, the words for gullible fool, sucker you know. And I spell it for him. Don't worry, he'll look it up. I know the type. Ah it was perfect, perfect. He doesn't know, you see, how much I meant it, how much of what he was saying I comprehended totally. He doesn't know if I am foolish or joking or lucky. All his certainty gone. Ha ha ha ha. Hoffnut."

"Oh Papa!" But she was laughing with him and was elated, too. "You're impossible," she said. But what did Hoffman expect, that Esteban was some ordinary slobbering old man?

"We'll celebrate," she said. "I've been tied to a desk all week and I want to get out. Let's have a picnic snack, out at Mt. Schyler Park like we used to do. Get some air. Do us both good. We can take something to work on and work with clear heads. Just like we used to do years ago. We can take some of the notebooks Alice has typed up. Let's take some of the early New York ones. You get them, and whatever else you want, and I'll go tell someone on the staff."

"Ask permission you mean?" Esteban said.

"Yes." She laughed, but with him. "All right, yes. From old Half-brow." And she left the room smiling still.

But permission was not so easy to get. She did have to see Hoffman. She could not just tell a secretary. And Hoffman was against it. In his office, behind his desk, he seemed a nice, sensible, rather heavyset man trying to do his job, and some of her elation left her. He did not want Esteban to go out.

"I don't see why," she said. "How do you find him, then? Isn't he doing well? Doctor?" she added, switching sides.

"I find his condition discouraging and deteriorating, frankly, Doctor."

"You have to make allowance that he has always been, well, eccentric. He's always liked his little jokes."

He waved all that aside. There went Leon Esteban, his wave said. "No no, I'm not talking about that," he answered her. "He's showing difficult signs. We feel, we have found, that he needs very careful handling. More than I think you realize."

"What exactly do you mean?"

"A phase comes over him now and then when he is extremely excitable and frenzied. He gets difficult. I mean physically, Doctor. We have all come to recognize it. We call it his hyena phase."

She hated him. For his accuracy. It was true. She had seen it herself. She had seen it the night they were boxing his notebooks and he had said she enjoyed it too much. Yes, she had. She had seen it, but she had not named it and so had forgotten it. Now she would always know it. No, it was too horrible. She refused.

"I don't agree," she said. "I don't agree at all. You've forgotten how depressing this place can be to someone used to a quite different life. You don't realize how confining, I mean intellectually of course, it can be for a man like my father. He needs to get out more. To be free of nurses and staff and administrators. I think he should be taken out much more. I feel I have been very remiss in not having done so before. I am sure it will help him."

"Where do you want to take him?"

"I thought I'd start with a little picnic in Mt. Schyler Park. We used to go there frequently."

"You want to take him yourself? Alone?"

"Of course. Oh, Dr. Hoffman, he's a tiny old man. Come now."

"I am against it. Absolutely against it. But I don't feel I can refuse you if you are set on it. I do insist, however, you take my car. Yes, I insist. It's equipped for such purposes. It has two doors only, and both have special locks which are difficult to open and which are set down low. I'll show you how they work. I insist that you take it."

"What took you so long?" Esteban asked when she got back. He was fully dressed, standing, and plainly fretful from waiting.

"Silliness," she said.

"They didn't want to let me go, did they?"

"It just took time to get some arrangements made. You know how these places are, Papa. They excrete red tape."

He became more relaxed as they left the white stucco building. She had been right to take him out. She was sure. She kept talking as they walked to the car and got in, and apparently he attached no importance to the change of car. He rode beside her with obvious and excited pleasure. And he looked so nice. She felt ashamed that she had not taken him out long before.

They reached the park after about a half-hour drive and she paid the fifty-cent entrance fee and started up the low slopes of the mountain. Clara intended to stop at one of the lower picnic areas, but Esteban asked her to go higher. He wanted to see the scrub cedar where it was thick and smelled good, he said, up near the top.

"All right," she said, and turned the car and began the winding drive upward.

"Go way up," he said. "That's right, to the little parking place just below the peak. It's not a steep drive, Fidélia."

She jumped, startled, but his face was blank, unnoticing. He gave no sign of the slip. There was nothing sharp, nothing crafty in his face.

At the topmost picnic area, where it was rocky and there was dense scrub cedar, she drove the car gently off the highway, bumping slowly over the rough half-rock half-grass terrain, and stopped as close as she could get beside one of the picnic tables.

"Hmmm, I love the air up here," she said. "I haven't come enough. We must do this more often." She got out and began unloading the little basket of food and utensils and the notebooks and papers he had brought.

Esteban got out too, walked slowly around the open picnic area, and then wandered over to stand by one of the little green cedars, seemingly with his hands buried in it. She had taken all their things out of the car and was trying to arrange them on the table in some order, aware she was never as neat as he.

"Well," she said. "I don't know if we'll get any work done here, but it is nice. You know I came up here once on a geology field trip. That was a long time ago. We were hunting fossils. They brought us in a bus and parked it down at the first picnic area, and we had to hike up the rest of the way. You know I'm terrible at that sort of thing, and after a few hundred feet I was panting like a haying machine. At first I was one of the ones in the lead, but gradually everyone went past me. Two of the boys tried to haul me along, but finally that wouldn't do either. We'd come to find little fossil snails and sea animals. All things that could be found here because of the fault that runs this side of town. Well, I'd had it. I couldn't go a foot further, dragged or not, and I just sat down on a rock

and gasped. To hell with it, I thought. I could hear
them all marching along, higher and higher, and I sat
on my rock gasping and staring at my feet, and right
there, between my feet, were fossils." She laughed at
the memory. "I found as many fossils as anyone. They
went scrabbling all over the mountain, in and out
among bushes, and I just sat picking up fossils from
between my feet. You know, I should have brought a
couple of blankets, or an air mattress. This bench is
going to be hard after a while."

He was still standing almost into the branches of
the cedar. Smelling it? Holding it? Good Lord, could
he be urinating in it?

"Shall we have something to eat first, or do you
want to go over some of these notes?"

"No, no. Fidélia," he said.

"Papa. You know I'm Clara."

He smiled at her. A sweet smile at first, but with
something sly developing in it. It stayed on his face
too long. And he was standing so far away from her.
Halfway across the picnic area from her, and halfway
behind that bush. Was he playing a game? Or what?

She sat on the bench. She opened a notebook, then
another one. But she could not bring it off. She could
not read them. He was watching her.

"I'm Clara," she said again.

"Don't worry," he said. "Don't worry. You were
always such a worrier. You were always afraid I'd
make a mistake in a paper. Change this, you'd say,
change that. Look out, Papa, look out." Mimicking
her voice and a little earnest nodding gesture of her
head. Oh, he was good at it. "This might be wrong,
Papa. Or that. You were good at finding my mistakes."

"It was how we worked," she said. "You wanted
me to do it. You didn't even want me to go away to
New York. Remember?"

"Remember?" he mimicked her. "No. You liked finding the mistakes. You were one for measurement, and you liked finding the mistakes." He was relishing the hurt.

"That's not so, Papa." She stood up. Instantly he was around the bush and farther away from her, with the little scrub cedar between them. He peered over the top of it at her, watching her, his eyes liquid and shining, pouring out malice from the sharp, the hyena face.

"Look, Papa," she began. Then, "Let's eat."

"Look, Papa," he said. "Let's eat."

"Stop it."

"Stop it."

She could not stand the way he looked, and took two quick steps toward him, but he flitted away, completely out of sight this time. She had lost him. She rushed, ran, to the bush, and on then to the next one. But her high heels (why had she worn them? But every time she had gone to see him, every time, she had dressed up, had dressed in heels and stockings and a pretty dress), the useless heels slid and lost traction and threw her off balance and she skittered to a stop. She could not run. She could not possibly catch him. Where was he?

"Clahra," he called.

She turned her head. He was across the picnic area. On the other side, near the car. How had he got there so fast? Thank God she had automatically put the key in her pocket. From just this side of the car he was watching her.

"Professor Esteban," she said sharply.

"No no." He laughed. "No no no. I wrote that one, remember? *Systems of Approach and Treatment*. Esteban and Holloway. Page 328 of the revised edition. Ha ha ha."

"All right. Papa then. Help me, Papa." But he shook his head, threw off the plea, and watched her, waited, expectant and still.

She began walking in his general direction, but not directly toward him. Moving instead so she might be able to cut him off if he started back for the scrub cedars. She had to get him. He could so easily get hurt here. He could fall or get lost. He was a small old man, no matter his fancy clothes or his quickness. She came closer to him, but he laughed and moved back to keep a bush between them, and there he stood, poised and waiting and expectant again, watching her over the top of the bush. If she could get close enough she could reach over and grab him. The scratchy little stiff branches would give way. She could reach through them for him. Again she walked closer to him, but slowly. She was beginning to perspire. Deliberately she slowed her pace, broke it up, made it irregular, but moved closer.

"Bye bye," he said, and ducked his head, bent over, and was gone from sight. She rushed after him, quickly quickly, teetering on the high heels, trying to cut between the bushes and perhaps surprise him. Quick quick, cut him off, get him. And she slid again, stumbled, and caught herself only by grabbing a limb of one of the cedar bushes and hanging onto the green bristly thing.

"Hell," she said.

There was a noise beside her. She raised her head and just above her—he must have been standing on a rock—was Esteban. Right there, on the other side of the bush she was holding. He was delighted. Delighted. He stuck his face forward between the bushes, with his eyebrows arched and his eyes wide, in a pantomime, a child's exaggeration of surprise. "Peek-a-boo," he shouted in her face, and jerked back, doubled over, and was out of sight.

In despair and rage she crashed through the side of
the bush after him and so suddenly that she saw him,
stretched out her hand for him as he ran doubled
over, crafty, animal-like, and she almost had hold of
him, almost had him, and then her heel caught and
held this time, in the scrub bush, and she was thrown
forward and down with the full force of her plunge
after him, and she crashed hard onto one knee, crying
out.

Silence.

Then, "Oh oh oh," she said.

"Are you . . . all right?" she heard. An old man's
voice. An old man's weak voice. "Clahra?"

She did not answer. No reply to this plea and pre-
tense of sanity. Shaken, hurt, bleeding, covered with
dirt, her stocking torn, trembling all over outside, she
was like marble inside, cool and hard and one piece.
Watching her blood ooze through the wide scrape on
her knee, through her ripped stocking, coming up like
red grass out of the brown torn stocking, soothing
and holding her knee, rubbing the hurt, rocking back
and forth and watching the blood, she knew her
father was an old man deranged in his senility. Was
mad. "Oh oh oh," she said, rocking her knee, holding
it. "Oh oh," but saying it automatically, for inside she
was still and certain and calm. From her pocket she
took a Kleenex and sopped the blood, sopped and
sopped it. "Oh oh oh." More blood. Oozing blood.
And it was Esteban who had written, *Remember how
ancient and how deep is the fear of madness, of this
terrible derangement of our very selves. Illness, even
death seem natural to us. Part of the life of the body.
But insanity, in all forms, comes as a foreigner rising
in our own blood, and is the more horrifying because
of the very intimacy of its strangeness.*

Slowly she stopped the ooze of blood. Slowly her
outer trembling ceased. The blood, the dirt on her, her

weakness, her apparent hurt, these were her weapons now.

Slowly, slowly, with great fatigue and great difficulty, barely able to do it, she pulled herself up and moved over to sit on a rock. There she sat, hunched forward, a lump of despair and hurt and shattered strength. She did not answer his two or three callings of her name. She did not look up when he came nearer. She sat.

Slowly she reached into her pocket and brought out cigarettes. Slowly, shakily, she fished out one cigarette. Then dropped it, reached for it, couldn't lift it, and began again fumbling for another. Finally she got it out, tried to put it in her mouth, seemed unable to do so, and rested, both arms limp on her legs, head down, too weak to smoke. Again she put the cigarette in her mouth, raised her head, and began searching clumsily for a match, first in one pocket, then in another, then back to the first.

"You have a match?" she said.

"Oh yes," he said. "I am allowed the tiny sort." And he approached. Was it going to be this simple? No. From a few steps away he tossed the packet to her. But he did not step back. He stayed. She seemed hardly to notice where the matches had fallen. Then with great slowness and fatigue, she reached down, found them, dropped them, got them again. She lit one, and it went out. She lit another, it held, and with it finally she got the cigarette lit. She inhaled slowly, deeply, then let her head slump down as before. Exhausted. Helpless. The sun blazing on her.

"Want one?" she asked him, her voice dull, indifferent.

"Oh no," he said. But still he did not move away. He shifted back and forth, standing first on one small rock and then on another. More and more restless. It was no fun now. She sat. He moved back and forth,

this rock, then that one, then this one, but all within a
tiny space, like a butterfly. More and more quick and
restless. "Oh no no," he said. "I am not allowed to
smoke. You should know that. I'm surprised at you.
You wouldn't really offer me a cigarette, would you?
You should know better."

She poked at the dirt with one hand, paying no
attention to him. She was slumped so far forward it
seemed she could not even see him.

"You wouldn't really offer me one, would you? Are
you hurt? Not if you can smoke. You should give it
up. It's bad for you. Why don't you give it up? It poi-
sons the entire body. You may already have cancer.
Do you know that? Do you cough much? Women are
susceptible to it, too. Especially women of your build.
On the heavy side. You should lose some weight. I
never put on weight. Smoking is bad for your eyesight, too. You have very bad eyesight, Clahra. You
can't see nearly as well as I. I can see far better. I have
perfect eyesight. You can't see that line of trees across
the valley," he swung his arm out to point at them,
"but I, I can make out what kind of trees they are and
I can see, in among them, yes, I can see some, oh,
some, let me see—" and in that instant she was up
and had thrown herself forward and on him, arms
and body spread around him like a net, springing and
jumping on him all before he could no more than turn
his head around toward her in surprise, and then they
both went down, clumping together onto their knees
with her arms wrapped around him. She had him. She
had him and held him fiercely. Such a frail little old
man, a thin bony little man. Yet she stood up and
jerked him with her, holding and handling him more
roughly, she knew, than she had to, but she was not
able to stop. She turned him around and tugged down
his jacket, the lovely pale linen jacket, until it was halfway down his arms, pinning them.

"Ah, Clahra," he said. "Too much. It's melodrama. Your timing was good, but don't do this, it's silly."

"Stop it. Stop that," she said. "Don't pretend you're joking. I'm not Hoffman, and you stop pretending you're playing a game. It won't do. You have to have help, Papa."

"Ha ha ha ha ha."

But she would not let herself mind. She took him to the car and put him into the back of it, and reached across the seat to fasten one lock and then through the window to lock the other door. Probably Esteban could open them. Probably he had invented the locks. But it would take him time to do it and she would be able to get back to the car before he got out. She gathered up the picnic lunch, the books and papers and shoved them into the trunk. Mustn't leave anything in the car for him to throw at her. Then she unlocked the door, got in, and settled herself behind the wheel, leaving Esteban in the back like a prisoner. It was terrible, but it was safe, and it was right. What if he had come to harm through her? What if he had been hurt because she had been stubborn and insisted he was perfectly competent? Thought he was joking! She would never have forgiven herself if some harm had come to him through her.

"I'm sorry, Papa. I have to make sure you aren't hurt. You understand that. I know you do. Papa?"

He sulked and would not answer. She turned the rear-view mirror so he could not find a place to sit where she could not see him by glancing at it.

"Who was Fidélia?" she asked.

He would not answer.

"Come on, Papa. Talk to me." But he would not. He sat in the middle of the back seat staring with venom at the back of her neck. So they rode, in silence, back to the Home.

Once there, as they drove into the parking area before the stucco building, he became more cheerful. When she helped him out of the car he asked, "Is it about five?"

"Just four-thirty," she said. She let an attendant take him to his room, and she went to sign him in.

"Have a little trouble?" Hoffman asked, distinctly pleased.

She was dirty. Her hair was down. Her knee and stocking were crusted with blood. "Yes," she said. "But it was nothing that I couldn't handle."

"All the same, you better not take him out again."

"No," she said.

She insisted on taking care of Esteban and helping him change his clothes, and she sent the male nurse out of the room. But Esteban refused to put on his pajamas and robe. "They always want me to do that, to prevent it, but I won't do it, I won't," he said. He was near bursting into tears, and here, where he was safe, among his books and papers and the books that he had written, seeing him nearly crying she lost all her inner firmness, and she let him do whatever he wished. She helped him select and put on one of his fine suits.

"Now," he said. "Do I look all right? Is it all nice?"

"You look fine, fine. But why the blue shirt with it?"

His face turned crafty and he smiled slyly at her and stroked the shirt with his fingertips.

"Wear what you want, please," she said. "Shall I tidy some of the books? Wait, where are you moving that chair? It's heavy."

"Here. Over here, with the light, in range of . . . of . . . it," and he nodded at it. The mirror, he meant. "Here in its focus," he said. "Hurry, hurry, little one, it's almost time."

"Time for what?"

He looked all around the room, first at the door and at each of the two windows, and then he said, lowering his voice and with his eyes and face hyena sharp, "Closer. Now listen," he whispered, "Fidélia." (Oh it was not her name. And it was not one of the names he had called her when she was small and her hair still fair and eyes, he said, that were green, and he would pick her up and rub his nose on her and call her his little golden penny, his little green pine tree. It was not even the name of her mother. It was not the name of anyone she knew.) "Listen, they mustn't hear. They try to stop me, but they can't. They'd find mistakes . . . ha ha ha . . . but on Sunday, and sometimes special during the week, I speak to the whole world. Me, I'm on," and he nodded at the mirror, "on TV."

Her mouth, her eyes broke wide in dismay. Oh Papa, oh dear God, oh it was so usual, it was so mundane, so unoriginal, so common, oh dear God, it was so trite.

He was watching her, greedy for her amazement, her awe.

"Well, I . . . I . . . uh, Papa, I. . . ."

"Shh, shh, quick," and he seated himself in the chair, very erect and proud and stiff, the mirror reflecting him in profile. He pulled, tugged on her arm, pulled her down, saying, "You must get out of range, get out of range, yes, yes," the *s*'s hissing. "Soon it starts, soon I will be on and you can see it, yes, yes," and from the corner of his eye he watched his profile in the mirror. "Any minute now, see," he said to her. So proud. "Well? Well, little one?"

"How nice. It's nice. It's great for you," she said, for he had written, *Don't argue with the old.* "Do you like doing it?" she asked, for *Indulge the senile,* he had said in that book that was the textbook of their science. "What . . . tell me what . . . oh God, what channel are you on, Papa?" Hadn't he written, *Allow them the pleasures of their sad fantasies, for how shall it harm you?*

Oh Papa, no, you were wrong, it's not like that, it's not, it's not.

"Lower," he said. "Down lower," pulling her arm.

"Papa," she said. "Shh, shh," he hissed, still pulling on her arm. "Papa," she whispered, "Papa," and her head came to rest against his sharp and bony knee, his hard old bony knee. "Shh," he said, "shh, shh," but gently now, soothing her, petting her with his hand, stroking her hair with his hand over and over again, tenderly, automatically, abstractedly, his mind elsewhere.

Angels

Patricia Lear

This day is the sweetest day. Other days you have to maybe tear up the place to find the bliss that this day has, its arms stretched out ready with warmth to jacket around thin shoulders, all right under Phoebe's nose, right under Phoebe's window, with her lying thin-shouldered and rolled up in a shivering ball in the up-stairs bed.

This day speaks to Vernon, though—and he listens, he thinks about things. Vernon, who has his large self artfully arranged in a light sunshower on the front steps of Phoebe's house—right under Phoebe's nose, right under Phoebe's window—spooning up some yogurt with Phoebe's one angel-wing spoon, raindrops making sequins on his little cap of hair.

This day, it is morning still, Vernon is doing his work-break thinking on Phoebe's wooden steps, steps that would have to be worked on at some point, he can see that, as there are chips and dissolving parts rotting in the corners and nutty bugs with see-through wings that fly up and stick in his eyes.

The house looks bad, the steps look bad, but the day seems to have something good in it, something almost healing in it, and Vernon is thinking he might go inside if Phoebe does not show herself soon or make herself known like she does by crashing around in the kitchen. Vernon might go upstairs and hustle her sweet prissiness out of bed and prop her out here with him so she can get some of what he is getting from this amazing day. He can almost actually do something like that with Phoebe now. They might actually be mixed up with each other enough for him to knock on her door and make a simple suggestion.

Vernon has learned all the neighborhood sounds. There are decibels loaded with meaning. Things rumble, some only under his feet. Vernon can, more often than not, tell what is coming down the block blocks before he can actually see it. His very bones are re-tuned now from the previous house where he was working before. His bones are tuned up and working for this falling-down house where if Phoebe were really smart, if she had half an inspiration, she would just toss a match in and walk out, pulling shut the door.

The dog is selective. The dog barks, but not always. Sometimes the dog lets things come down the street and right up the driveway to the house and stays quiet while staring point-blank out the window. The part of the dog's routine that is a routine goes like this: The dog barks at the mailman but not at the laundry man. He barks at the UPS truck but not at the Chemlawn Service. And always, you can bet on it, the dog is apoplectic at the garbage men, who come up the driveway like a SWAT team.

The dog does not bark at Vernon anymore—maybe a couple of woofs. And after Vernon and the Chemlawn and the UPS people and the rest of them that are predictable entities, all dog routine is tossed out the window. What the dog does is a matter of the dog's mood or of how good he has been sleeping or if one of the cats has been giving him a hard time or if the position the moon was in, in the night sky, let moonlight fall across the house at an evil slant.

Vernon has gotten so he just lets himself in in the mornings, Phoebe staying in her room with the talk shows before showing herself girlish and waxy-skinned and smelling sickbeddish downstairs, her halter-top bandage looking faintly Grecian showing above where she wraps her robe with a sash. Phoebe doing what she has been doing lately: knocking things over going through the cabinets looking for coffee beans and filters or checking for cinnamon tea in the canister beside the cooktop, all the noises Vernon has yet to hear this particular morning.

Vernon spends time musing on the spoon, turning it over and over in his hands, feeling its weight, rubbing the handle with his bent thumb where the angel wings are worked in silver. He balances the spoon on his knee and it rocks there slightly while he is rocking the top off a second carton of yogurt. He digs his hands into a bag of raisins and rains some down, spilling them out his cupped hand over the yogurt before doing some movement, smiling to himself and doing something vaguely priestlike with the silver spoon.

Phoebe is standing behind him. He senses her now, and looking back, he sees her, her face up close to the screen of the screened-in front porch looking veiled, a face barely there. Vernon's beginning to know Phoebe's presence before he knows she is there.

"You sitting out there in the rain for any reason, Vernon?" Phoebe says, holding an empty Limoges cup, the cup an old wedding present from her gone marriage like the spoon.

Vernon will get around to telling her to throw out all the plastic ones, the dumb mugs with the cleaners' names, the banks' names, stuff she has no business with now. "The sun is out too, you know, Phoebe," Vernon says. "Come on. You sit down here beside me and feel Nature's sauna. I have to wait for the plaster to set up."

"Somebody might see me in this robe," Phoebe says, looking up and down the block. "And I have to stay inside for the water to boil to make coffee. You want some?"

"So let them see you then," Vernon says. "You need to sit and let the sun melt some of that crust off, darlin'."

Going back inside, Phoebe starts upstairs for something for her hair while holding the robe in her fist up from tangling in her ankles. Sighing so she can hear him, Vernon follows inside and busies himself with rinsing the spoon at the kitchen sink and with wiping it in a paper towel to lay it out on the countertop for Phoebe to use, it being the only piece of silver she will get out, the silver too beautiful for anything crazy— such as using it. Vernon tosses the empty yogurt cups in the garbage and dries his hands, thinking that given what life can be, some things are a blessed shame. Given what life can be, you better get out your whole silver service if you got it.

Vernon is plastering in the dining room, so he would have to be deaf not to hear the crashes— Phoebe, her hair in a thin ponytail, standing in the kitchen pulling down coffee beans and other things from the top shelf, opening and closing the refrigerator, talking to the animals while she opens a can of cat food for the cats, pours some dry dog food into the dog's dish, grinds up coffee beans for herself, and slams her way around, busy in a way that makes Vernon gradually begin to forget about her altogether, his mind coming back to his own drifting thinking, such as to when he can find time to work on the steps.

"Were you in my room?" Phoebe says. "I kept dreaming you were in my room," she says, leaning up against the door to the dining room, her arms crossed over her chest, and holding now a full cup of coffee in the Limoges cup.

Vernon is mixing up another bucket of plaster with a long pine stick, turning the stick mostly two-handed and sometimes making a little flipping move with one hand, flipping the tiny Louis Vuitton purse he wears over his shoulder to his back again and again but never taking it off. "Nope. Thought you should be getting up, but no, I wasn't coming in to see if you were still breathing."

"How can you call yourself a construction worker when you wear that stupid purse?" Phoebe says.

"Sweetheart," Vernon says. "Phoebe, sweetheart, maybe we do ourselves a favor by not calling some things anything." She smiles for a moment. "Anyway," he says, dropping the stick into the bucket and executing a sweeping turn, "I am not a construction worker. What I choose to call myself in my real life is an actor. This is not my real life." Then he walks from one end of the dining room to the other and circles back again. "I could teach you to model," he says. "You are thin enough and have a look. It would give

you the most fabulous life, Phoebe, the life of being a
model. If I weren't such a pig, I would do it. If I
weren't such a pig."

Suddenly, surprising Vernon even, Phoebe slips her
hand in his and pulls him through the house, Vernon
jabbering, "Now what in the world are you going to
do with me? Just what?" She pulls him back to the
steps, where he crumples into a slouch again, his
purse dangling off his chest as she is stepping her narrow body over his, which, in the skirts of her robe,
Vernon sees flashing past his head, her toes bright
with polish from some night of TV. Phoebe crawls herself headfirst on her hands and knees into the wild
part of the yard, where the shrubs and plants and
little trees and brush are woodsy and left strictly off-
limits to any lawn-care efforts.

She fits herself back in with the bushes and says to
Vernon, who adjusts his body slightly to see her better,
"Tell me something, Vernon. What ever happened to
the simple man in the paneled truck? Where's the
handyman with his box of tools who does his work
and just sends the bill?"

"Oh. Okay. I'm getting it," Vernon says. "I'm understanding you now," he says, lolling his head around
and loosening up his neck, little flying bugs fanning
out around the back of his head. "Well, just remember
this, sweet pea. Remember this—you called me. I
didn't call you. So come on and at least stick your legs
out in the sun."

Phoebe sits up on one ankle, crossing the other leg
over her knee, and folds herself into a Buddha shape
deep in the brush. "I hate every minute. Every minute," she says.

Vernon shrugs. "Okay. Fine. Stay out of the sun.
Sun's bad for your skin. Everybody needs good skin,"
he says. "I need good skin," he says to himself, fumbling in his breast pocket for a pair of sunglasses

while Phoebe rolls this way and rolls that way, looking around on the ground to see if she is sitting on
anything besides leaves and weeds and dirt, something
like maybe a slug. Finally, she straightens up and sits
quietly picking things off the palms of her hands.

Vernon watches for a while, then stares off down
the block to where he had felt the mail truck was
going to be coming up over the horizon pretty soon,
and now the mail truck is actually doing it; coming;
now stopping, right a few blocks up on Phoebe's street.

Phoebe and Vernon wait.

The dog climbs the front steps and scratches to get
into the house. A station wagon goes by and hands
trill out the windows. A bumblebee powers around
the planter box as Phoebe and Vernon wait, gently
lulled into that morning lull where the mail is on its
way. Phoebe and Vernon wait, in a lull, for the
mailperson who is not there, not there, not there—
then is there, is here! suddenly, is all at once finally in
view, the mailperson dressed in summer shorts and
traipsing, kind of dancing down the block, working
her way from house to house.

Vernon calls out to Phoebe. "Crawl on out here,
Phoebs. Here comes some more get-well cards and
your new *Rolling Stone*."

The mailperson makes her way up Phoebe's front
lawn, shifting her mailbag from one shoulder to the
other while Vernon fidgets with getting his purse
squared with his belt buckle, while Phoebe is stepping
her way barefooted back deeper into the bushes, her
robe gathered up in a wad in her lap.

The mailperson stomps one hiking boot up on
Vernon's step, then does a thing to get her hair up out
of her face. She pulls earphones from her ears and
gives Vernon a grin.

Vernon glances over at Phoebe, who has a cat stepping over her lap going one way, then turning around
and stepping over her going the other way.

The mailperson kisses towards Vernon with glossed
lips, so Vernon kisses the air back at her. She digs out
the mail and hands it to Vernon, so Vernon kisses the
air at her again. Still grinning, the mailperson fixes her
earphones back in her ears and goes off down the
yard in the same way as she came, dancing, sort of
gangly, slinging her bag back up on her shoulders on
her way toward the neighbors'.

"She is leaving now, Phoebe," Vernon says, standing
himself up on his feet.

Phoebe unfolds out of the bushes, the cat plunging
down off across the yard.

"Some things are really an experience," Vernon
says, wondering off after the mailperson, with Phoebe
musing too. "Some things just knock me out."

This day later, early afternoon, Vernon's van, with
Vernon driving Phoebe, is going along silhouetted
against the sweetest, smoothest sky. When he hits city
traffic, Vernon drives his van coasting and gunning
and keeping to the slow lane, mostly staying trapped
behind a city bus, even stopping when the bus stops
and going when the bus goes. Coke bottles roll back
and forth on the floorboards. Candy wrappers are
wadded on the seats. Phoebe, in an old slidy raincoat
somebody left in the front-hall closet, is kept from
going through the windshield by the seat belt Vernon
let loose as far as it would go and strapped over her
balled up body.

"Man," Phoebe says, heaving sighs.

Vernon is playing the tape he just bought on the
tape deck and is beating on the dashboard, leaning for-

ward from time to time to punch either the fast
forward or the rewind.

Phoebe shakes her head.

"So, your-highness-queen-of-the-universe, what do
you think?" Vernon says. "Good tunes? Whew! I like."

Phoebe looks out the window.

"Oh. Okay. I get it. You want me to go up there
with you? I will go up there with you. Do you want
me to?"

The road ahead opens up. The bus turns off. Vernon begins working his way through traffic, coasting
a little, then gunning, then coasting, then gunning
again to arc too widely around several cars and an am-
bulette, next double-parking in a towaway zone in
front of the professional building in the middle of the
huge city hospital complex. Phoebe climbs down out
of the van and stands looking back at Vernon through
the open window.

"Okay now, Phoebe," Vernon says, "Listen here,
Phoebe. This audition will take about two minutes for
them to throw me out on my butt, so then I will come
back here and wait right here out on the street for
you. Right here this way or down there that way, but
I'll try for here, so when you come out, be sure and
look both ways, you know, both up and back down
that way. I can't say what the parking situation will be
when I get back here. By then."

"We deserve better," Phoebe says, Vernon nodding
solemnly and saying, "Baby, baby, baby. Yes indeed,
baby." Then Phoebe turns and goes up the walk.

Later on this blessed day, as early afternoon becomes real afternoon, no more lulls like with the mail,
Vernon is parked out in the van doing breathing exer-
cises. He does stints of holding his breath and raising

up so he can look out the window to search the faces
paddleboarding through the revolving door, a thing
that makes him headachy, so he gives up on his exer-
cises and picks up an old parking ticket to read that
has been dropped with the bottles on the floorboards.
He thinks about the lunch wagon he saw parked just
around the corner and thinks about dashing over
there for a bite. But there is always the chance that
Phoebe might paddleboard herself out of the professional building and forget how she ever got where she
is and wander off to get herself a taxi home.

"I am here to tell you that there are many, many
things that can hurt," Phoebe says to Vernon through
the window as she is trying to work the door handle.

Vernon jerks his head up, his arm resting on the
back of the seat. "Hold on. Let me get that," he says,
springing into action.

"Let's trade places, Vernon," Phoebe says, getting in
the van. "I got to drive. You have to let me drive because I need to have something to do with myself
right now. I have to run this one last lousy errand."

Shifting her over by sliding her across on top of
him, Vernon says, "Phoebe, believe me. Phoebe, from
the bottom of my heart. We all go through things. We
all of us go through things."

In the parking lot of the department store where
Phoebe has her errand, she stands shoving up and
dropping down the sleeves of her raincoat while
Vernon circles around locking up the van. He buckles
his knees to spit-shine away a dirt spot that turns out
to be a door chip.

As they go in through the cosmetics department, silvered tree branches arc over their heads and there are
lead crystal vases filled with peacock feathers sitting

on the glass counters. Vernon hypers around trying to find the escalator, to find the store directory, while Phoebe moves slower, moves along peacefully browsing the counters. She stops to rub an anti-aging lotion on the back of her hand and to watch a how-to makeup videotape. She takes a perfume sample from a pretty woman in a cocktail dress holding a little hill of them on a tray.

Vernon spots a sign offering a gift box of candy just for today, just for opening a store charge account. He wanders nearby to the little gilded desk manned by a charge-account man and digs out his driver's license and a couple of credit cards. He reaches for a pen. As Vernon glances over at Phoebe, which he does from time to time, he sees that she is mostly just working her way along the counters messing with testers or looking at what's in a free-gift-with-purchase package. Later, when he glances at her, he sees something new; he sees Phoebe locked in a gaze with herself in a mirror, one finger raised, barely touching her face. And with her free hand, she is raking her nails through her wind-knotty hair.

Vernon reaches for the box of candy and goes to Phoebe, slipping his arms around her from the back. Then he takes Phoebe and walks her, the two of them together, to a counter with more of everything, with the unusual as well as the usual, with tiny bottles of glitter suspended in clear gels and a vivid bank of testers stair-stepping up next to a column tied with the silvered tree branches.

"Okay," he says to her, flipping his purse over his shoulder. "Hold still and I will do you. Yes?"

Vernon works loose Phoebe's top button and in soft, loose folds drops the slippery raincoat down off her shoulders. He uses his thumbnail to break the cellophane on the box of candies, then hands them back to Phoebe. "Here is lunch, sweetness," he says to her as she begins to settle nicely under the pressure of his hands cleaning her face with astringent-soaked cotton balls.

Then picking up a piece of candy from the box, Vernon crushes it slightly, then puts it back, then picks up another and crushes it, and then finally he feeds one to Phoebe and eats several himself. "This is nice," Phoebe says, searching around in the box. Vernon puts his hands on her head and holds her still, bringing her face up so he can stare intently into her eyes. "Okay. I got it," he says.

Rubbing a cream into her damp skin, he says, "SPF of 15. Always use an SPF of 15. But then you already know that. I don't have to tell you that. Jesus, I need to tell myself that."

He reaches for a small sponge and next works in a pale foundation, one shade lighter than Phoebe's skin. He fluffs her face with fine-milled rice powder and buffs the powder, bringing her face up to a satin finish. Standing back, he studies her for a moment, crossing his legs at the ankles and looking in the mirror and back at Phoebe, going back and forth, Phoebe moving her face to the mirror and back along with him.

Vernon then studies the candy box for a moment. Brown pleated candy wrappers are scattered all over the counter. He collects himself up, sighing, choosing a small brush, and starts in on Phoebe's eyes, first brushing her brows up with a little dark powder; then using his fingers, the brush, and the fat part of his thumb, Vernon works a whole palette around her eyes, using colors in a layering fashion, some matte colors, some metallic colors, some just no color, just brown and just almond, these shades all going up to her brow and spreading out from the corners of her eyes.

"You okay?" Phoebe asks.

"Me?" he says, pausing to push back a few loose dangles of her hair. "Me? I am the handyman. Of course I am okay."

"Well, I, for one, dare I say it? I am having fun," Phoebe says. "I love the chocolates. This is all very nice, Vernon. Very sweet."

"Well, look at you, Phoebe-bean! Angel-wing eyes, for God's sake. And having fun too. Listen. Tell me something, sweetness. And tell me true. Do I look old or what?" he says, bringing his face close to Phoebe's and leaning his shoulder into the curve of her bare shoulder. "This part's serious."

"You look good, Vernon," she says, beginning to fidget, getting her arms high enough to hold him off. "Sort of youngish. Medium-young old."

"Everything I want you have to be young for," he says, returning upright.

"Everything I want, you have to get old for," Phoebe says, leaning around to see herself in the mirror.

"Well, what do you think of that? We should trade then," Vernon says, pulling her raincoat up from around her shoulders, and shaking it up in little shakes to glide evenly over her shoulders. He kisses her on the top of her head, smelling her hair with the kiss, and twirls away from her, saying, "Okay, Phoebe McPhoeb, I only care about the eyes. You do your lipstick any way or no way at all."

He begins to put some color on his own face, to edge his own eyes with a fine pencil line. "God! Jesus, I just am seeing myself," he says. "Well, do as I say and not as I do, baby-cakes, you know—about the sun."

Phoebe busies herself with testers, running colors across the back of her hand. She picks out a screaming bright color for her lips. "Now I want to buy all this stuff," she says to Vernon. "Now I have to own all this stuff."

"Oh, good God no, certainly not, heavens no. Absolutely not," Vernon says. "That is what the Walgreen's is for. You ever go to the Walgreen's? The shampoo aisle alone—"

"How do I look?" Phoebe says, slipping off the chair and turning toward him.

Vernon walks a few steps away from the counter, then comes back and picks up the chocolates. He works at fitting the top back on the box, but the little pleated papers are springy and will not go flat.

"How do I look?" Phoebe says.

Vernon looks over at her and heaves a sigh. He offers out his arm for her to fold into, her standing there not moving, her arms hanging at her sides, the raincoat skimming her body.

"I am exhausted, Phoebe," he says, heaving another, even deeper sigh. "So let's go find the tit lady and get this thing over with."

They wander aisles, ride the escalator, make a stop by the drinking fountain while working their way back to the lingerie department, even at one point going back past the charge-account man, who lifts another box of candy at Vernon. "Oh, tit lady, oh, tit lady," Vernon calls. They work their way back to where there are racks and racks of nightgowns and robes, camisoles and other underthings, Vernon nudging Phoebe along, her saying in different ways the same thing, Phoebe saying, "Oh, this is just beautiful. That was a wonderful way to put it, Vernon. I am just loving every bit of this myself. Come on. Leave. Go. Let me go alone."

Vernon keeps the two of them going, steering
Phoebe along by keeping one of his hands firmly on
the back of her neck, all the while with the other hand
fingering the different materials that they use for these
kinds of things, flipping his fingers through fragile
laces that stir around, that ruffle a bit, and then blowing on other things that puff sleepily up in the air and
then drift back down before sighing into silken folds.
"No way. I'm seeing this thing through to the end."

Phoebe says, "Whatever *did* happen to the old days
when the handyman arrived in a paneled truck and
then left and sent the bill? What *did* happen to the
nice fellow who got himself up from J.C. Penney?
Now we have designer purses. Now we have involvement."

"Listen, Phoebe," Vernon says, "Give me your
hand! Give me your hand! Listen to me, Phoebe.
There's not all that much involvement. I am doing
your house, and when your house is done or when
you run out of money or when I get bored out of my
skull, whichever comes first, then I'm doing somebody
else's house. That's still the bottom line, just like in the
old days with the paneled truck."

Vernon dips close to a freestanding designer trunk-
show rack of drippy chiffon. "It's all about money,
chimichanga," he says, maneuvering his head so something mistlike is passing over his forehead. "And when
I get my shit together, then I'm doing nobody's
house—would that that day would ever come, oh
God, please, come, come."

Phoebe, seeing him veiled in this way, smiles and
juts up a shoulder, which nudges him so he stumbles,
having to grab hold of the rack and step clear through
to the other side to keep his balance, all the while
dragging her along behind him. Gowns that slip easily
off their hangers are drifting to the floor, and Phoebe
and Vernon, anxious with trying not to get their

makeup on something, with not pulling the whole
rack down on top of them, anxious with trying to
keep upright while all the while they are falling with
the utmost of care that they can muster and even
some grace, Phoebe and Vernon fall along with the
gowns and negligees and peignoirs and bed jackets, all
of them top-of-the-line designer-expensive, all of them
strewing around with Phoebe and Vernon, all of them
going down on the floor rumpling up together.

Vernon sighs and gently lies flat down on his back
on the store linoleum squares and stretches out his
arm for Phoebe to rest her head on. From the things
still hanging, delicate creamy laces stream a muted
light and glowing satin ribbons loop and trail into soft
folds on the floor.

Vernon looks up at the pipes on the ceiling and
Phoebe watches feet walking up and down out in the
aisle.

"Oh my God," Phoebe says.

"Just use some old socks. Forget the lady. We'll get
you a whole pack of sweat socks at the Walgreen's.
Just stuff them in something, you know."

"Where is the candy box," says Phoebe. "And will
you please quit saying 'tit lady,' Vernon, you faggot."

"I did not this time say 'tit lady.' You are just react-
ing all on your own as if I did, and also I cannot even
look at you eating those things anymore," Vernon
says, shoving the candy box out into the middle of the
aisle.

Phoebe rolls over on her stomach and looks in
Vernon's face.

"Angel-wing eyes," he says. "I am a hell of an artist, Phoebe. Look at you! Actually, you look like hell.
Just kidding."

Phoebe reaches up behind his head and checks the
price tag of a gown lying on the floor. "You look
worse than me. Just kidding. No I'm not."

"Phoebe, sometimes I get the strangest feeling. Sometimes I get the feeling you are giving me your death."

"Hear that, God? Vernon is volunteering the ultimate. What a guy."

Vernon adjusts his arm a little and looks up at the pipes on the ceiling. "The sleaziest, the very sleaziest—"

"Well, I guess you could just add it to your bill, couldn't you, Vernon," she says. "Like with the paneled truck? But I think you have your life and your death and I have mine and that the two don't have a thing to do with each other. Not one thing. Wish they did. Wish they did."

"Okay, well, are we having fun yet? That is the thing," Vernon says, rubbing Phoebe's back since both his arms are wrapped around her, with her relaxing on top of him and dangling her arms down off his sides. "What are we going to do? What are we going to do, baby, baby?"

More people walk up and down out in the aisle. A lingerie lady comes and begins adjusting the rack, Phoebe and Vernon lying silently on the other side. Soon the lingerie lady goes away, calling out for some woman named Ethel. "Ethel, Ethel," she says.

"Go to the Walgreen's?" Phoebe says, unfolding herself and beginning to untangle her arms and legs from Vernon and disentangle herself from a bunch of silky things. She starts to get up off the floor.

And Vernon, standing up along with her and working his way free of a peignoir, then getting his purse untangled from where the strap was close to strangling him, says, "Well then, give me your hand, Phoebe, and we'll go where we can get us a better deal on body parts."

"Not here," Phoebe says. "You sure not here?"

"And show some dignity getting out of this place, girl," Vernon says.

"You really dying for me, Vernon? Hey, Ethel, he's mad for me, he's practically dying for me."

"Shut up. Walk, Phoebe," Vernon says. "Come on, just hold my hand you little tarted-up—"

"Angel," Phoebe says.

The Stockholm Syndrome

Maxine Chernoff

It isn't right for a woman with one breast, a woman that anyone would call matronly, to go on vacation, meet a man, and never come home. That's what Clarice did last summer, and all I have is a postcard to hint at a reason. I blame Buddy, who made her life difficult at home. She once told us why the book club never met at her house. "Buddy doesn't want his privacy invaded," she apologized, jokingly. Maybe he would have to throw on a clean shirt for us or help Clarice serve the refreshments. Maybe he would have to say more than hello. Not that he was a bad kid, but he was a kid for too long.

Clarice would come to our book club meetings prepared, ready as anyone to discuss whatever it was we were reading. One week, long before it became a movie with that sad sack William Hurt, it was *The Accidental Tourist*. Clarice was the presenter, which is how we work it. We take turns. One month Shirley does it, one month Irene, one month it's me, and then

Clarice. It's no little thing to be a presenter. Irene, for
one, gets a new dress when it's her turn. I remember
one Tuesday last March when she looked radiant. It
was her turn to lead us in *The Life of Patty Hearst*. I
for one wouldn't trade Patty Hearst's millions for her
rotten life. But that's another story. Irene's wearing
a black rayon suit with little white dots by Nina
Piccalino. But what I remember most is how passionate Clarice got defending the girl. She said she might
do anything for a lover like Patty Hearst did. We
asked if he'd have to lock her in a closet, and she
said no. There's just a time in your life when things
are right to do, and I guess when Clarice went to
California was one of them.

She was sixty-seven, which means that Buddy's
thirty-seven. Now I believe in strong family ties, but
Buddy's not a regular kid. He's been known to take
advantage. I've known Clarice so long that I remember Buddy as a child. Kids can get clingy when a
father dies but even before Abe passed, it's Buddy
needs this and Buddy needs that and Buddy can't do
this or that for himself. That's why that particular
book club on *The Accidental Tourist* is so memorable.
Clarice is in the middle of making an important point
about one of Macon's brothers. Shirley's in the middle
of disagreeing, and the phone rings. It's Buddy. He's
locked himself out of the house, and Clarice is supposed to leave the book club to let him in. We can tell
she's embarrassed. The discussion isn't half over, and
she has to excuse herself because a grown man can't
hold onto his keys or hang out in a bar until she's
expected home. She says it won't take more than
twenty minutes and she's right. At 2:20 she's back,
and I really must commend the way she picked up the
discussion right where she left off. The sad part was
that we were about four chapters ahead, but nobody
had the heart to tell her.

One of Clarice's arms is always swollen from the operation she had some years ago. She's a thin woman with a pretty face and clear blue eyes. We call her Einstein, not because she's a genius but because of her hair. I bet when she was little, someone was always telling her to fix her crazy hair. It's the kind of short hair that looks long and wild. She has a nice figure and dresses well. You can't tell except for her arm that she's had the breast removed. I can see how a man would be interested in her face. She'd usually wear full sleeves, but sometimes she'd see a nice suit or dress and just buy it. If she can live with her arm, anyone should be able to. I wonder if the man she met noticed the arm or not. I think about it because Clarice is shy, and I worry about their first time in bed if he didn't know.

She sent me a postcard of Chinatown after she decided to stay in San Francisco. Now years ago I was in that same Chinatown with my husband. We were in a restaurant that serves dim sum, those little dumplings with different fillings, and damned if a little Chinese girl doesn't pass us with a cart full of cooked duck's feet. They are as yellow as the sun, and one of my little ones, Andrea, screams. She was a real sensitive kid. If she saw a bug smashed on a windshield she'd cry. Having three brothers didn't make it any easier for her. One of them was always hurting something, by accident of course. If there was a cat around, its little tail might get slammed in a door or if there were goldfish maybe one of the boys would leave the bowl in the sun on an early September afternoon. Their water would get so hot they'd be cooked by the end of school, and poor little Andrea would come in and discover them. So it was really too bad that even on our vacation she couldn't get away from it all. Clarice never sent photos of duck's feet. She sent a bright red pagoda, and the message was short: "I'm so happy with Keith that I've decided to stay." Well, if she's happy I'm happy too, but getting that message made me wonder. You'd think she might have called, but sweethearts like their privacy.

When the postcard came, I phoned Irene. I wondered if we should visit Buddy and inquire after his health. Here's a boy, a grown man really, but every creature comfort has always been given him. He gets three square meals a day and a warm place to sleep. Putting it that way makes it sound like he's living in a kennel, but you know what I mean. He doesn't have to struggle like the rest of us. Clarice has some money, Buddy has a good man managing his dad's old business, and things are fine. Maybe he meets a girl now and then, but it's never serious enough to replace Clarice.

First Irene says we shouldn't meddle. If Buddy's unhappy, Clarice is sure to know. But I say it's the kind thing to do. Suppose Clarice died. Wouldn't we look after Buddy for her? From Buddy's point of view, Clarice's moving away might not be much different than her dying. So Irene agrees. If I call Buddy and he wants to see us, she'll come along.

I try reaching Buddy for about four nights without much luck. It's a Friday night when I finally get him on the line.

"Buddy," I say. "It's Mrs. Riess." Not that I'd mind him calling me Margaret, but he's always called me Mrs. Riess.

I hear him turning down the television in the background and saying hello at the same time. He doesn't sound all that glad to hear from me.

"Irene and I were hoping you're fine. We wanted to say hello." He doesn't say a word, so I'm going on like this. I even tell him the story about the duck's feet before he says much of anything.

He asks me how my kids are. I give him the summary, though I spare some details about Andrea's divorce. That's a topic I try to avoid. It's better for my health. I ask him if he needs anything, and he says he would like to talk to us, meaning me and Irene, and says why not come by tomorrow about four.

When I tell Irene that he wants to see us, I'm surprised at how she reacts. She has no curiosity or confidence, I'm not sure which. She says in her twitchy little voice that Saturday's really a bad day for her, and she already has plans and about a hundred other things that don't make sense. She uses up every alibi she's ever contrived for this one meeting with a boy of no consequence. I tell her I'll go alone, and she says she promised to go and will try to live up to it.

I've known Irene forever. Even when we were kids, things used to intimidate her. There was a teacher who was crazy. You could have had Miss Nichols certified. It terrified her to be touched. She'd shout things at children like, "Look what you've done! You've made a run in my stockings!" when someone stepped on her toe. We'd intentionally jostle her just to see her face turn red and her eyes get small with anger. But not Irene. Irene spent fifth grade watching extra carefully where she stepped. Once as a prank Bobby Roeder pushed Irene into Miss Nichols.

"We should watch where we land!" Miss Nichols screeched, knowing full well as a teacher that objects crashing through space don't have a will of their own.

Irene honks for me at 3:45. I'm already out on the porch waiting. I've bought some bakery cookies to take Buddy, and Irene, the one who doesn't want to go, has baked a marble pound cake. It's sitting between us on the front seat of her Ford. Irene's a slow driver, so we arrive about twenty minutes later when it should take ten.

We wait a long time at the door before Buddy answers. I expect to find a mess in the house, but the front room's immaculate, and Buddy's laid out some fancy pastries and nice mugs for coffee. He's ground the coffee in a special machine, and it smells much better than the instant I've come to use. Buddy seems to have a house guest too, a nice younger man named Dave. Dave is in the kitchen when we come in, and his sleeves are pulled up to his elbows, and his hands are in the sink. He's washing dishes. It's not remarkable because men are different these days. They take care of things if they have to.

We sit in the front room. Buddy and I are on the couch. Irene's in a light blue easy chair, and when Dave finishes in the kitchen and we're still making small talk, he joins us too.

"Nice of you to come," Dave says, like we're here to see him, and I begin to wonder if Dave is more than a friend.

"Do you hear from your mom?" I ask Buddy.

"They talk all the time," Dave says. "You should see our phone bill."

The way he says "our phone bill" clears a few things up for me. "I bet you're glad to have Dave around now that your mom's away," I tell Buddy.

I look at Irene, and she's digging a hole in her coffee cup with her spoon. She won't look at me no matter what I do.

"Dave lived here before Mom left," Buddy tells me. "She's happy out there, and I'm happy here."

"So everybody's happy," I add. I look around the walls of the room. There's a lot of Indian art and some is frankly erotic. I wonder if Dave's an anthropologist. "So what do you do for a living?" I ask him.

"I'm a dog groomer," he says. "We met when Buddy still had Bridget." Bridget their poodle's been dead for almost a decade. I know that because Bridget died before Rudy, my little collie.

"And you've lived here all these years?" I ask.

"Only a few months," Dave explains. And he shoots this little smile that's only meant for Buddy through the room.

"Have you met Keith?" I ask Buddy.

"The mysterious Keith? No, but he sounds very nice on the phone. He's a retired math teacher. Do you know how they met? Mom went to a Scrabble club, and they played each other in a semi-final round."

"Who won?" I ask, and Buddy says he doesn't know. I think it's strange that he doesn't know the outcome of a story he must tell again and again, but some people are just naturally curious and some are not.

Now Irene, who's been as quiet as can be, pipes up. She doesn't say she likes their furniture or anything normal. "I think it's the Stockholm Syndrome," Irene says.

Plunk, the words just lie there. She's back to stirring her coffee and choosing another pastry. I know what she's talking about, but does she expect me to do all the explaining?

Finally Dave says politely, "Excuse me, but what's that?" It figures he doesn't know about the Stockholm Syndrome, being a dog groomer. It's not like a dog groomer can't listen to the news, but he probably doesn't go in for the big issues like me and Irene and the rest of us in the club.

Of course Irene doesn't answer. There's a moment of silence that makes everyone flinch, and then I say, "It's when captives fall in love with their captors. Like Patty Hearst having a love affair with that man who raped her."

The men exchange glances. I bet they don't expect old women, friends of Buddy's mother, to talk that

way. I wasn't trying to be shocking. I was just trying
to explain what they asked.

"So you think my mother's being held against her
will?"

"Pardon me," I say, "But I was just elaborating for
Irene."

That puts Irene on the spot so she pipes up for
once. "This man beats your mother, a very good Scrabble player, and then they fall in love. It doesn't have to
be physical, how people overpower you. Keith subdued your mother, and now she thinks she loves him."
Her mouth snaps shut like an electronic door.

Two things come to my mind. Dave and Buddy
haven't asked why it's named after Stockholm. If
either of them was really thinking, he'd have asked.
And why is it that Irene thinks Clarice lost at Scrabble? No one said a thing about her losing. "Buddy,
did Clarice lose?" I ask.

"She didn't say." Then he's quiet for a second. "But
if she didn't say, I'd guess she did lose." Buddy and
Dave share a big laugh because they've thought of the
same thing at the same time. I remember laughing like
that with Norman before the kids were born. I try to
smile at Irene about Buddy's conclusion, but it's not
the same.

I see that it's getting late outside and these two men
are probably busy, so I tell Irene we'd better go.

"Why do they call it the Stockholm Syndrome?"
Dave asks before we're out the door. Hoping Irene
will do some of the work, I'm quiet. We stand there
still as statues until I say that Stockholm's the place
that hostages go to get deprogrammed. Buddy makes
some joke about a clinic that breaks hearts, and we all
laugh at that. I don't know if Stockholm's a romantic
place, I'm thinking, but there are all kinds of love,
that's for sure.

Dave shakes my hand and then takes Irene's hand in his to say goodbye. Watching Irene's tentative smile, I think of crazy old Miss Nichols.

As soon as we're in the car, Irene sighs. I'm used to her making that same sigh after sixty years, but it says so little that I'm wondering why she's satisfied with it anymore.

I Miss Saturday Night

Eleanore Devine

For Alice, Blanche, Helene, Mildred, Lenka, Florence, Mary, and Jeanette who lived part of this story.

Martha walked through the Old Orchard Mall as if everyone who had ever cared for her lay in wait across the street in Memorial Park. In a dark place full of young and laughing people, she had a martini and a hamburger. A man passed her table, a man bleached with age the way Tom, her second husband, had been. His blazer was like Tom's and his gray flannels lay slack over his buttocks. She ordered another martini and sipped it until the young people began to dance. By then she had missed the last bus and had to ask the bartender to call a cab.

Her daughter Carol was waiting at the new kitchen table she and her husband Josh called "an island." At her feet, Delsie, her prize poodle, slept, legs moving on the black tile floor as if she were swimming.

"Mother, I worried."

"Because I hadn't made dinner?"

"Listen to what I'm saying. I said I worried."

Martha's hand moved out flat and sharp to dismiss her daughter's words.

Carol's hand rose to block her mother's gesture. "Everything I do, you push me away."

Martha slumped to a chair and plunged her fingers into Delsie's fur. The old dog answered with a sleepy snuffle.

"Mother, pay attention for once. I'm fighting for my professional life. I'm doing the best I can to help you, and you walk around as if Josh and I beat you."

"Let me be." Again Martha's hand moved out flat and fast.

The next morning Martha turned herself in at the Senior Center. (Tom would have liked that verb.) To the first person she saw, she said, "I'm bored, being wretched."

Her counselor's name was Judi. Martha had lived so long with hurrying people, silence like a shroud, that she wasted no time spilling her guts. (The phrase was Tom's. He said only women did it.) Later she would have liked to tell Carol about Judi—"Her hair stands straight up, as if she'd poked a finger in an electric outlet, but under that hair, she's smart." Her daughter never asked.

"I'm not the mother my daughter wanted," Martha told Judi.

She continued, "I have every symptom in *The Merck Manual*, pages 414 through 463. That's heart. Not to mention pages 944 to 5, hearing loss."

Judi asked, "Have you considered the reasons for your symptoms?"

Martha said, "I lost two husbands, the man I'd always wanted to marry and part of my heart. My hearing aid squeaks. My new teeth spit."

Judi nodded and hummed, took notes and smiled. "Tell me about your daughter."

"My daughter-the-geriatric specialist? You must know about her. She has all the answers, but she can't slow down so I can understand what she's saying."

"Do you know why you and she are so angry at each other?"

"Yes," Martha said, and cut off the question. "Her husband runs the busy track too. He goes to New York and gambles with time to see how long he can linger with a drink and a girl he doesn't want and still catch a taxi and his plane home. Their son—my grandson—the maid fed him, dressed him, babied him so well he flunked the entrance exam. Kindergarten.

"Now he's in a program that gives him a B.A. in two years so he can get on with his M.D."

Judi's laughter, low and warm, more of a murmur than a laugh, startled Martha. "I was not aware," Martha said, "that I was telling jokes."

"It's the way you tell your troubles."

Martha laughed too and their laughter merged in perfect complicity until she said, "Maybe I can explain again to my daughter how to talk to me. I hate not knowing what's going on."

"You can try," Judi said.

That night, her bœuf Bourguignon in the oven, Martha tuned the TV to Bill Moyers. She couldn't understand what he was saying, but she liked looking at him. His voice sounded the way maple syrup smells. Beyond the TV, the window was open; the scent of geraniums mingled with the thyme and brandy, red wine and garlic of her peace offering. Suddenly Carol was home. She bumped her mother's chair as she passed, turned down the volume, slammed the window, leaned down and said, "Mother . . . neighbors . . . noise."

Martha said, "If only you'd lean down to me more often, look at me and not shout," but she still could not say it aloud.

Later as Carol worked her evening crossword puzzle, Martha said, "You could still learn to talk to me."

Carol poked her pen into the word she was working on and ink spread in a blot. "Not now."

"Now."

"I don't feel like talking now."

"What does that ink make you think of?"

Carol did not answer.

"Bad day?" Martha asked.

"Yes, we'll talk at dinner."

Dinner was like all the dinners: Carol and Josh talking, Martha watching.

They were a handsome couple. A glint of silver in their hair. Good bodies. They jogged together every morning, each with a report on hemostasis on his Walkman. Now, eyes tight and bright on each other, hands touching, they spun out their words, faster and faster, brighter and brighter. Martha felt anger in her daughter's voice.

"Josh, I told Doctor . . . *New England Journal* . . . I told him . . . I explained . . ."

"Carol . . . I agree . . ."

Sitting at their table, nibbling her beef, Martha wanted to be happy that her daughter and son-in-law cared for each other, that they were proud of each other's work—what happens, chemically, to old blood and bones. They were discussing a professional crisis, Carol's professional crisis. At last, modulating her voice as best she could, Martha spoke. "Please slow down. I can understand if you look right at me. I love all the details."

"We're talking about my boss, the clod." Impatience twisted Carol's lips. She turned back to Josh.

Watching the two of them, alone together, Martha saw her daughter as she had that morning so long ago. Even as a child Carol never had time to knock on doors; and so, one morning, there was her daughter looking down at her over Tom's shoulder. Carol's eyes were hugely black behind new glasses; braces cramped her mouth; but there was peach bloom on her cheeks and her black hair shone in a thick braid. She was already dressed for school. She was saying, "Mother, you haven't even looked at my report card," and Tom, sliding slowly deep inside, had shouted, "Get lost, kid."

Now, Martha quit trying to read Carol's hands and lips. She knew what to do: Get lost.

Martha visited her friend Margaret who had inherited three trust funds and could live as she wished. Margaret had chosen a complete care residence, Still Waters, as in "He leadeth me."

"I need people," Margaret said. "With a companion, I'd be isolated. And she might hover."

Martha said, "Dread words. Hover. Linger."

Still Waters had a three-storied lobby, striped Empire-style sofas and a $75,000 fountain that sang, "Plink-plink-splash-plink." Margaret and her friends had new hair-dos and manicures.

"Maybe even facials," Martha told Judi the next day. "There's a beauty parlor in the basement. They sit by the fountain, do needlepoint, and say, 'What?' One of them tats. I haven't tatted since I was ten.

"The building committee spent three years finding
a bachelor architect, an only child, who didn't know
that running water induces urination. That's why
the sofa covers are plastic. Depend, Inc. paid for the
fountain.

"Micturition Manor," she said, her hand moving
flat out, flipping up, a joke now for Judi.

She said, "Tom's favorite name for a nursing home
was The Kiss of Death. I don't have that kind of
money, but I probably won't live long."

Judi helped her get a HUD apartment: Two rooms
with a Pullman kitchen, shelves for her Willa Cather
collection, and a closet for scrapbooks, her three
skirts, four pantsuits, and twelve blouses from Field's
Junior Miss department. Judi gave her a red rug,
sheets, and a card table with three chairs she claimed
she was about to take to Thrift House. Martha
bought a La-Z-Boy chair. She looked at futons.

"You can't sleep on a futon," Judi said, and then as
Martha's hand moved in protest, "O.K., you can *sleep*
on a futon, but how are you going to get up in the
morning?"

Judi talked her into buying a captioning machine
for her TV so she wouldn't disturb her new neighbors. Margaret sent a five-foot Peace Lily. Her card
said, "Before Wally was a duchess and the duke came
to call, she rented palm trees to fill in the empty
spaces." The day Martha moved, Carol and Josh were
in Geneva at a world health meeting.

Martha invited Margaret and her friends to lunches.
No one did dinner any more. She learned to sit on a
stool in the tub and soap all over, then rinse her hands
before touching the guard rail. Judi taught her to put
her pills in small plastic cups: Two blues and a white

for breakfast, three pinks for lunch, a blue and a yellow for dinner. A young woman Judi recommended took the squeak out of her aid.

Every Tuesday she received a hurried call from Carol. She was never sure what her daughter was saying, but as Carol called Judi once a month to ask how her mother was doing, Martha got her family news second-hand: The doctor who had blocked Carol's progress had moved on to Mayo's. Josh missed his plane at Kennedy a month ago. The catch-up-kid was an intern in Hawaii.

Mostly she was alone.

She talked to herself.

She knew what she was saying.

She never closed the blinds. At night she lay on her bed by the window and stretched her arms and legs fifty times. Tom used to say, "My left leg's giving me fits." Hers did spasms and jerks. She tried not to think, "What will I do when I can't walk?"

Gwen, down the hall in 209, couldn't read newspapers any more. Most mornings Martha read the *Trib* to her.

Lying there, remembering, she watched the trees dance against moonrise. In the distance was a scrap of Lake Michigan's quicksilver. She planned to tell Judi, "I've better recall than a computer."

Night, upstate Vermont, rain and flood, lightning like the finger of God, hell's own rain, she and Pa piling up stones they would never again be able to move. Water thundered against the dam, then poured into her parents' fields.

The dappled gray she exercised after school on the end of a long rope, round and round, hour after hour, day after day, until the mare let her mount.

In the dome car heading for L.A. by way of Feather River Canyon, watching the train curl through a

mountain pass ahead, she patted Tom's thigh. He said,
"Watch it, public place," then, "I'm lucky."

"Me, too," she said.

Lying there, on her very own bed, she felt his lips
between her thighs.

She tucked a pillow under her breasts and slept.

Mornings, she woke with stone hands and feet. Her
heart thundered and pushed against her chest. She
flexed her fingers and toes and tightened her sphincter
muscles twenty-five times to prevent incontinence and
to firm her vagina, an organ she'd never need again.
Sometimes, as her friends shouted above the splish-
splash of Margaret's fountain, she pretended Tom was
there and squeezed inside.

She watched the sun mount the sky.

She was no longer lonely alone.

By eight, her promises for the day gave her strength
to get up. She'd agreed to go with crabby old Janet
in 201 to the hospital and come back by way of the
library for the large-print romance Gwen had request-
ed. People here needed her. Sometimes their children
or grandchildren came to her rooms and told her their
problems.

She got a Senior Pass and took a bus, almost any
bus, to the end of the line and back, watching neigh-
borhoods she'd never known go by. Once, seeing The
Guild, a book store she'd always wondered about,
she got off. Ferlinghetti was there. She bought a small
yellow book of poems for $2.95 and he autographed
it. On the bus, she read, "I feel there is an angel in
me . . . whom I am constantly shocking."

She explored new shopping malls and tried to figure
out who the people there were, where they were going
and why. She pretended to shop for furniture. Life-size

bronze horses. No dappled grays. Sofas with wide stripes and purple pillows. She looked at thigh-length dresses with a bow and a ruffle at the hem, skirts like panty girdles. As she wandered, she laughed at the small person she saw in shop windows: Face wizened as an apple-doll, white drip-dry hair, a chiffon scarf and red pantsuit. Her lipstick matched the suit; it was too bright for her face, but only she knew that under her suit her breasts sagged and her bones grew lumpy.

She pretended there were small springs behind her toes and walked with a bounce. She practiced funny stories to tell Judi. She savored the joy of going home.

Evenings she read.

She said to Judi, "That Isabel in *The Portrait of a Lady*, if only she'd do something, even tat. James says she's an intellectual. He shows her holding a book, but she never opens it."

One Saturday evening, early in September, Willa Cather's "Old Mrs. Harris" seemed to be written in a language Martha no longer knew. (On Monday she'd said to Judi, "Cather should have called that story 'Proud to be Put Upon.' ") Martha closed her book and began to pace back and forth. Up the hall in 201, Janet would talk about her laboratory tests. In 207 Dottie would bring out her grandbaby's pictures. In 209 sweet Gwen would discuss gardening. Angie, one floor up, would argue Mapplethorpe's right to photograph his concerns.

By her window, massaging the back of her neck, Martha watched the sun glint on her beloved patch of quicksilver. In the sudden emptiness that was her home, she said, "I miss Saturday night."

Saturday nights she and Tom went square-dancing. They traveled. They won prizes. She had long hair that bounced with the music and fifteen petticoats.

Even as a toddler, Carol had treated her new daddy like an uninvited guest. Later she complained Tom was mean to her. In seventh grade, she said, "Mother, you never stand up for me."

Now, Martha said to her daughter who was at a medical meeting somewhere, "I'm not rewriting history. Tom wasn't a good parent, but he made me laugh. His steps matched mine."

Monday Martha would report to Judi, "My brain feels too heavy for my head."

She chose a red sweater from the closet, took the elevator down and stepping slowly, watching her feet, turned east in the early dusk toward the canal and the lake. No need to fall flat out and scrape her nose as she had the week before because she had been curious about the wooden frills three carpenters were adding to a tan bungalow.

Ahead, tiptilt on the sidewalk, was a small red, green and white plastic tricycle. The year she'd married Tom he'd ordered a bike custom-made for Carol from one of his manufacturers. It was red and white, maybe the first bike made after the war. Carol had screamed until Tom removed the training wheels. By the third day she was riding. Tom said, "That kid, she's going to be the first underage female USA president." The next week, someone stole Carol's bike. Martha lifted the plastic baby-trike and put it over the low front hedge.

On the canal bridge a young man in a white shirt and a woman in black leaned into each other. A moon full and soft as a peach rose above the Baha'i Temple. At beach parties, she and Tom used to sing, "Shine on harvest moon . . . for me and my gal." He had a strong baritone. She quavered along.

Across Sheridan Road, houses, link-metal fences, hedges and flowers blocked the way to the lake. She moved up a long driveway and came to a gate. The cinnamon fragrance of pink petunias and the pee-smell of a certain kind of spruce—she'd forgotten the

name—engulfed her. She picked a sprig from the
hedge. She would look up the spruce when she got
home. A sign on the high wooden gate said, "NO
TRESPASSING."

Softly, as if from far away, a dog barked a nervous
warning. She reached out to steady herself and felt its
body batter the gate. She had raised dogs on the farm.
Delsie had gotten cross in her old age, but to the last
she had climbed in Martha's lap and comforted her.
She would quiet the strange dog; then, her hand on its
collar, they would walk to the lake. But people might
come. Lights flash. A burglar alarm sound. She
touched her ears. No aids. Judi often said, "I know
you're upset when you forget your aids."

If the police came, she would not understand them
in the dark. What could she say?

"I need the lake? The lake belongs to everyone?"

Years ago, their fragile-faced postman, the kind
who marched weekends to save the redwoods, used
to walk through Tom's hedge. In those days she never
shouted. "But this is our ecology," she explained.
"This hedge is our greening for America. Please
respect it." The man would nod and, branches
cracking under his feet, crunch on through.

She turned her face to the smooth planks of the
gate. Her head seemed to hover over her left shoulder,
then swirl over the barrier, over the lake, on its own
like a balloon caught in an updraft. The dog's frenzy
increased. Time to go home. Time to have done with
explaining. She'd never been good at it any way. Monday morning she'd tell Judi, "They gave me the gate."

On the way home, she watched the moon's path
widen on the canal. Clouds gathered at the horizon. A
flash of lightning warned of rain. The young couple
stood tight against the gray railing. She felt their bodies join, sweet and strong, the way it was when she
first knew Tom.

✦ ✦ ✦

She undressed and pulled her red comforter to her chin. Her hands smelled of spruce. She lay and watched rain beat against the windowpane.

She said, "Good night, Tom."

She said, "Carol, I wanted you to be a happy child."

Then, quick as the lightning, a sharpness ripped her chest. She passed a hand from breast to stomach. There was no blood. On the table at her side was the button she was supposed to push for help. Life was inches away. Her hand moved out flat and slow— inches short.

Vibrations Which Rumble Like Thunder

Anne Brashler

Her husband is in the next room, rapping his knuckles against the glass tank, spooking the Dempsey, the aggressive fish he's learned to hypnotize. She could visualize him using the handle of the green net to chase the Dempsey out of the weeds, its blue specks on dark scales shining while the back of the Dempsey's body lightened until it was shades paler than the fish it intimidated. Protective coloring; law of nature, law of the jungle, law of the universe. She permitted one floating image of the darkened room in which her husband hovered, the ninety-gallon wall tank with neon lights casting an eerie glow on green plastic plants and rocks of blue and red. The loud thump was her husband stomping on the floor, making, he thinks, vibrations which rumble like thunder waves to the Dempsey, the Silver Dollars, other fish trapped in their glass cage.

It had been six months since she'd watched herself
and her husband move from their home in the country
and settle into this little house, the place feeling old
and used and battered by previous owners. While
she'd packed in the country home, she'd felt the distancing as she sealed boxes and marked the outside
with black crayon: bedroom, office, kitchen, shed.
"Distancing" was stepping out of her life while she
hovered above the person packing and moving down
below.

At her former home, frog sounds broke through the
silence of night while early morning woodpeckers
tapped out rhythms on poplar trees. They'd lived in
the country home for twenty-three years, raised a
family, watched the children grow, leave home, spawn
families of their own; then sold the house to the
Polanskis, a family of nine in need of more space.
They would leave behind glass showcases her husband had built for his miniature circus carvings, a
riding lawnmower, and Quaker Oats cans of emergency supplies in the fallout shelter.

When the Polanskis couldn't sell their house, she
and her husband agreed to take it on trade. "It's a
deal," he'd said, signing the contract. Since the closing
date was two months away, she, to her later regret,
suggested the new buyers move in gradually, thus
expediting things later on.

The new family came every day. As they pulled up
in their van, seven children swarmed across the back
yard, into her garden bed of wild strawberries, violets,
and buttercups. Mr. Polanski especially liked the glass
showcases and was pleased with the keys her husband
had given him for locking and unlocking. "Might start
a gun collection!" he'd said, but her husband showed
no interest.

As time went on she began to notice how Mrs.
Polanski imitated her way of doing things; settling

on wicker baskets, buying plants, asking for her
brownie recipes, asking how she made tacos and
quilts, and what neighbors she liked and didn't. At
first she considered the imitation a kind of flattery, but
then, when Mrs. Polanski began wearing similar
clothes and had her hair cut short, she felt as if she'd
lost part of herself. Just a thought at first, a string dangling from a loose button. Mrs. Polanski bought
Laura Ashley dresses just like hers and looked better
in them than she did.

She countered by wearing blue jeans and baggy
sweatshirts, the kind Mrs. Polanski wore when
she first looked at the country home. When Mrs.
Polanski asked about bird-watching, she said she
didn't notice any particular birds in the trees. "Just
those old blackbirds, is all," she said, hoping the red-
headed woodpeckers wouldn't start pecking away in
the poplar tree. She didn't mention pheasants either,
the way she and her husband used to scatter wild bird
seed in winter and how mothers and chicks paraded
up the hill.

During this time, her husband gathered his miniatures from displays throughout the midwest and
packed them away in cartons. He became so somber
while doing this, she wondered if he felt he was burying them. He'd begun the hobby long ago, spending
hours carving tiny horses, elephants, clowns, and
painting authentically scaled replicas from the Dan
Rice Circus.

Shortly after signing the contract, she watched her
husband climb the hill where pheasants gathered, his
back not as straight as it once was. She wondered if
he felt he was being replaced, the way she did. Was he
ready for Mr. Polanski's Flea Market and drinking
beer with next-door neighbors on Saturday afternoons? He'd talked about the fish tank Mr. Polanski
had left in the house then, wondering if fish could

take the place of pheasants. "We'll give it a shot,"
he'd said. "See what happens." She knew having fish
for pets would be something strange for him, a fisherman from way back, up in Rainey Lake in Canada,
the walleye going for jigs and largemouth bass going
for rapalas and northern pike—big enough to feed a
family—going for anything at all.

By the time moving day arrived, she felt as if she'd
all but lost her old self to this new woman who'd
taken her place. A distress she couldn't place hovered,
threatening. As she settled into a routine in the little
house, she lived mostly in the jeans and old baggy
sweatshirts, sometimes not bothering to remove
clothes at night but sleeping in them; it was so much
easier than putting on a nightgown. She scrubbed
fingerprints from walls, turned out lights in the crawl
space, threw away wigs she'd found in the attic. The
wigs were so filthy, she picked them up with paper
toweling, feeling a growing resentment toward Mrs.
Polanski who'd moved into her nice clean place.
"Darly," she'd say. "I mean, really!"

There were other things in the attic which she'd
wanted to toss, but her husband said to let them be.
"Maybe someone left something for each new owner,"
he said. "It might be important."

"Who'd want a Jesus light with Jesus wearing a lit-
up crown of thorns?" she asked but he didn't answer.

Before feeding the Dempseys live guppies, he now
slipped into a green elf costume he'd found in the attic, along with a dusty photograph of Mr. Polanski
wearing it. The costume had been made from a set of
men's longlegged underwear with a drop seat in back.
The green flap drooped on two sides where buttons
were missing. "Oh my God," she'd said. "You're turning into a wimp." She leaned into chores with a zest
that should have exorcised her growing anger toward
the Polanskis, but didn't. "I can't help it," she said.

And he'd answered, "Now, Sweets," in a way that made her enraged. He hadn't unpacked his circus display; the boxes were still in the shed.

When they'd moved in, the fish tank was coated with algae and slime, dark gravel that smelled like Limburger cheese. Her husband found overalls of Mr. Polanski's in the shed and wore them when he cleaned out the tank. She put away dishes, made notes of things she wanted changed, like the overhead lamp in the dining area—a composition of six balls which looked as if it belonged in the Algiers Motel on the corner.

As she made new lists of things to buy from old lists, her husband climbed a footstool to reach the bottom of the fish tank. He scooped up dark brown gravel with his hands, holding his breath until he transferred the gravel to a dishpan which he carried outside. "Smell must've killed the former fish," he said. He folded a handkerchief into a triangle and tied it around his nose.

"I know fish SMELL," she said, "but do they smell?"

He dumped the dishpan of gravel into an aluminum can, then rinsed the gravel with a garden hose until the water ran clear. "We'll use the can later for putting our garbage out front Sundays the way the neighbors do," he told her. Garbage cans, empty cartons, and bedsprings crowded sidewalks on Sunday afternoons like attendants watching a parade. He wore Mr. Polanski's overalls almost exclusively now in the daytime.

Their tiny home sat in the middle of others just like theirs. McDade's Catalog house with its neon signs, the block-long Jewel Food Store with fresh lobsters swimming in a tank, the OPEN ALL NIGHT gas stations, and the Algiers Motel made her feel as if she'd moved into a shopping center. She drew the drapes at dusk in case a passerby would mistake them for living models in a housewares promotion.

"Darly, do I look different than before?" she asked over coffee one morning.

"Before what, Luv?" he asked. "Before the hurricane? Before the flood? You give me no reference point." He returned to a full page ad on pet supplies, found feeder guppies at a bargain.

"Before you became a little green elf," she said. "Before the Dempseys and the Silver Dollars, when we were back at the old house."

"Nope. Same old gal," he said. "Want anything? I'm going to the pet shop." He was into fish now, all the way. Sometimes, when he stood close to the tank, spooking the Dempsey, he barked like a dog and wiggled his fingers in the air—which made the Dempsey head for a hole in back of the plastic plants. He spent long hours in the pet shop. "They sure spend a lot of time doing nothing," he once remarked to a customer in the store. The customer looked startled, then said, "What else are fish supposed to do?"

"Never mind, Darly," she'd said at the time. "He probably blew the tenth frame in bowling last night." She wondered if her husband, in time, would go back to his miniature circus carvings. He'd once been a dynamo, selling ideas rather than solid matter. "The sizzle, not the steak," he used to say, tracking down carpenter jobs in the city, out on farms. He'd learned the craft from his father. When his father died, he inherited the tools, set up the jigsaw and workbench in the bomb shelter. A successful contractor by then, with enough earnings to retire, he became a circus master of sorts, traveling with his miniatures in winter months, putting on shows, pitching out his razzle-dazzle in nursing homes and hospital rooms. Where was that hotshot now? Where was the sizzle?

After a while she "did" the house, buying a flowered bedspread, new wicker chairs and tables, painting walls, and changing carpeting in all the rooms, carefully buying 'baskets of such silken grace you felt them float from a table' as a writer once said, an Oriental rug for the living room. She drove to shopping malls, feeling strange at first in her new role. Before long she began to feel life stir, not quite like being pregnant but something like that, expectant. She kept drapes open so that neighbors could look inside and admire what she'd done. Sometimes the doorbell rang and she'd answer it, telling the person inquiring where she'd picked up this vase, that picture, those flowers. If they stayed, she served chilled wine and cheese as if having open house. The home began to feel like hers now, but she still blamed the Polanskis for her husband's change in behavior. She bought new display cases for the circus pieces, but he didn't bother to help set the cases up after they were delivered.

Once she stepped into the pace of her new life, she felt buoyed up by the different directions and choices open, a surprise like an unexpected gift.

She never used to enjoy shopping, but now she went almost every day. "Where're you going?" her husband would call from his post by the fish tank. "Out," she'd say and leave. She tried nagging about his circus still packed in boxes, but he seemed not interested. "Oh, some day," he'd say vaguely, brushing the air with his hand.

She had the fun of buying new clothes for someone other than Mrs. Polanski's persona. She threw her blue jeans and sweatshirt in the garbage can and was pleased to see them hauled away, ground in the iron teeth of the truck. Her new clothes were more expensive and happier looking than what she'd worn before. She discovered she loved soft wools and glowing graceful silks and found a dressmaker who measured and designed and advised. "Join an exercise class," the dressmaker said. "Keeps you fit. Get your hair done."

So she stopped shopping and let the dressmaker create her clothes and do her buying while she exercised daily at the Lovely Lady Salon. She jogged to rock and jiggled on the jiggle machine and rode a bike up a thousand miles of imagined hills. She closed her eyes to fill the hills with maples and oaks, the side of the road with goldenrod, sumac, and black-eyed Susans.

When she sang in the shower, which was every morning now, her husband shouted something about caterwauling, and she realized her distancing was gone; she'd come down inside her own body again. She went to plays in the city, driving by herself—something she'd never done before without her husband; but he wasn't interested in plays anymore. Wasn't television good enough? At least PBS? Or why not come and watch fish? He'd let her feed them if she wanted. He fed them guppies often, watching the Dempseys open their trapdoors and gulp the guppies down.

"They look as if they just suck them up," she said, horrified.

"Those Dempseys, they're all fish," her husband said.

At last she unpacked his circus pieces, set some on display in new cases in the living room, arranged a ring of clowns around a red-and-yellow striped tent on the coffee table, but he scarcely noticed. He still alternated between wearing the elf costume and Mr. Polanski's overalls. She washed the overalls at night after he went to sleep. "But why?" she'd asked when he wouldn't change into his own clothes. He'd answer "Oh, I dunno; makes me feel different, I guess." She played marches and circus music on the record player.

When she went to plays in the city, she'd call him so he could fix dinner. One time when she telephoned, he said, "You've got to come home. That woman what'shername, the buyer of the big house, wants to talk to you."

"What about?" She'd all but forgotten Mrs. Polanski.

"Don't know, but they'll be here in an hour."

"They?"

"Both of them. He wants to know if he can buy my circus. Seems he's taken an interest in woodcarving."

"Are you going to sell him the circus?" she asked, goose bumps rising on her skin.

"Don't know. Maybe."

"You can't," she said and hung up before he could respond. She hurried home and paused by her front door, expectant and frightened.

When Mr. Polanski met her at the door, looking exactly the way her husband used to—wearing the same type of gray slacks, a turtleneck sweater, even black horn-rimmed glasses just like his, she was terrified until she heard her real husband call from the room with the built-in tank. "The fucking Dempsey just swallowed a Silver Dollar," he shouted.

"Hi there," Mr. Polanski said. "Wanted to see the old neighborhood, wanted to see what you two've done. Didn't like our carpets, I see. Didn't like our color scheme, either, right?" He picked up objects, checking out trademarks. Before she could stop him, he knelt before the coffee table and swept up all the clowns. "These are really something," he said. "No wonder he didn't want to show them to me before."

She feared for the little clowns, so vulnerable in his hands.

Mrs. Polanski's Laura Ashley dress with blue forget-me-nots was dingy and wrinkled as if she'd washed it with blue jeans. She gazed with surprise and wonder,

eyeing the soft silk blouse and rainbowed skirt. "How
lovely," she said. "Where did you buy those clothes
and who did your hair?" This was not a friendly
neighbor asking about a wicker chair or a framed
print. Mr. and Mrs. Polanski swallowed people whole.

Get out, she wanted to say.

"I've chilled wine and the cheese is room tempera-
ture. Will you join us for a while?" her husband
asked. The green flap on his elf costume was down
again even though she'd sewn on buttons many times.

"Oh, they mustn't stay," she said. His empty circus
cartons lay sprawled by the front door. "Who dug
those out?" she asked.

"I did," Mr. Polanski said. "He told me I could,"
he said.

"They go, these stay," she said, pointing first to the
amazed Polanskis and then to the boxes. Her face became mottled with anger.

"But, Sweetie . . ." Her husband seemed embarrassed.

"But nothing," she said as she opened the front
door. "Sorry," she said. "My husband forgot he's
giving a lecture tonight. Kiwanis club, I think."

When Mr. Polanski tried to hold the door open
with his foot, she slammed it shut. "Goodbye!" she
called. "This is our home now!" She locked the door
and slid the dead bolt into place.

After getting rid of the Polanskis, she made a few
telephone calls, persuaded her husband to change into
his old clothes—with tie. When he protested, she
threatened to drown the fish, chop the miniatures into
kindling, then burn the house down.

They went together to set up his carvings in
Walgreen's twenty-four-hour drugstore. Insomniacs
and bag ladies watched as the druggist removed
end-of-season tackle boxes from display shelves to
make room for the circus. "Jeez," the druggist said,

lifting out the miniatures with care. "Just like the old days in Appleton, Wisconsin."

"Best circus in town," her husband said, clearing his throat. He bowed to the small gathering and looked as if he might topple over.

"Go for it, Darly!" she said, clapping.

He shrugged, seemed to come out of a fog, and then, "Step right up, Ladies and Gentlemen!"

(She smiled, relieved.)

"。. . and observe the Magnificent Marvelous Miniature Mysteries gathered here before your very eyes."

A group crowded around him as he hopped on an overturned carton, light as a feather.

"The World Famous Burberry Circus," he shouted. "A Private Presentation at Wondrous Walgreen's, the Friendly Family's Famous Favorite place to shop . . .

". . . A Monumental Modern-day Miracle, unchallenged in Size, Scope and Splendor . . .

". . . Terrific Terrifying Tigers, Daredevils Daring to Do Dangerous Feats on the Head of a Pointy Pin . . ."

She hung back, apart from the gathering, seeing her husband in his old tuxedo and top hat, swinging his cane, selling the sizzle. She'd put him in the window now, where everyone could watch. She stomped her feet on the brown tiled floor, making her own vibrations.

A Slight Movement of Hands

Joyce Goldenstern

He is practicing magic tricks in front of the stand-up mirror in the back room. I watch him from the living room. I'm trying hard to figure his tricks out. To understand magic. When Aunt Clara calls for supper, he is imitating Groucho Marx eyebrow grimaces and is searching his pocket for a cigar. He does not smoke them. He uses cigars only to make us laugh. I try hard not to laugh. He does not love my aunt. I found a picture of him and Lola on the top shelf of his closet. Kissing. Kissing. Not the way he kisses Aunt Clara. Aunt Clara is calling for supper. He walks into the living room which is lit only by the magic lights of the Christmas tree. Aunt Clara has turned them on. Aunt Clara has decorated the tree. She has put up the manger scene. Eva, my cousin, his baby, is touching the colorful boxes under the tree. Christmas will come in ten days. We wonder if he will be at home. Aunt Clara has wrapped the boxes. Aunt Clara has put them under the tree. He doesn't even know what's in them.

Roast chicken, buttered beans, and rice. Aunt Clara sits properly at one head of the table. She seems happy to see him for once sitting where he belongs—at the other end, across from her. She gives him the last piece of chicken. "Why give it to him?" I want to say. "Eat it yourself." Her good intentions, as always, only seem to make him irritable.

After dinner the coin trick for Eva and me. In the background, the noise of Aunt Clara's dishwashing. Then the surprise. A new trick ordered by mail. A plastic egg transformed by sleight of hand into a duck. Ruffled fuzz and feathers. Aunt Clara appears at the doorway which separates the dining room from the living room. A sad turn to her head. As the limp and lifeless duck appears in his able hands, Eva shrieks with pleasure. He looks at Aunt Clara with triumph in his eyes.

Eva and me tucked in the hideaway bed. We sleep in the living room. He kisses, teases, tickles us. Aunt Clara kisses us once on each cheek, makes us say a prayer. Eva falls asleep. The cars whiz by to bless our covers with their light. I make myself stay awake. Watch. Listen. Him and Aunt Clara in the back room. From my bed, I can see Aunt Clara's face in the dressing table mirror. Complete silence. I can see him stand up. Search his pocket for the cigar. Tiptoe to the hallway. Take his leather jacket from a peg. Slip it on as he walks out the door.

Gabriel, Gabriel, Lorenzo, Lorenzo. When he says his name whole, it seems a stuttering, a song. All my childhood, I hear the whispering and shouting of his name. Gabriel, Gabriel, Lorenzo, Lorenzo. Music. A sad echo. He smiles when he says his name, as though the name itself makes him special. "My saint's name is Gabriel, too," he explains. "And my mother married her first cousin. My mother's surname was Lorenzo and so was my father's."

"Incest," he says. I remember the smoky smell in the Catholic church. But that is not what he means.

"Cousins can marry," Aunt Clara says.

"Not first cousins. Look what happened."

"What happened is that they both died young. They left him alone."

"I am an orphan, too," he says to me. "My uncle raised me, too. Just like I'm taking care of you."

Him a little hoodlum boy. Walking the streets alone. Smoking cigarettes. Getting into fights. Stealing a car to ride around the block. Running away to America. Working in a factory. Going to school at night.

Gabriel, Gabriel. Yes, I find a picture of him and Lola on the dusty top shelf of the back room. He has letters up there too. Then I remember, though I had forgotten it, that he left us one winter, the winter after his knee operation, to go to Florida with Lola. Aunt Clara said he had to go to a warmer climate to recuperate. In the picture, he is kissing her on the mouth. I never see him kiss Aunt Clara on the mouth. Lola's hair is dyed blond. She sits on his lap.

Sometimes I watch him watch Aunt Clara—proper, precise, lifting a piece of roast chicken to her lips (painted red), her fork properly held in her left hand, and wonder why he doesn't love her. I wonder why it is the precise way Eva emphasizes the word "exactly"—"What is it *exactly* that you do Papa?"—mimicking her mother, sends him running to catch her in his arms. But the same voice in the mouth of the mother he hates. I love Aunt Clara. My mother's sister. I never show her the photograph. I feel sorry for her when she calls him at work to find out where he has been all night. I try hard to criticize his magic. I wonder why God has given him such a wonderful gift. I try hard to figure out his most difficult tricks. I try hard not to listen to his stories. Not to love him, in spite of myself.

✦ ✦ ✦

"You are special," he tells me. He starts to take me everywhere. But I know his tricks. No, I won't forget Aunt Clara. I won't forget. Your tricks are tricky, Gabriel. They do not make me laugh.

He takes me on the bus. One day to his job. One day to play pool. One day to watch a boxing match. One day to buy a Christmas present for Lola and her son. He begins to talk to me about Lola. One day he even takes me to her house.

Lola's son is Robert. He goes to my school. He has no father. He is possessed by the devil. That's what he says. That's what his mother says. He is ten years old, but he clings fiercely to her skirts whenever he thinks someone is watching or chasing him. "We are going back to Florida," Robert tells me. "There are good doctors there."

"They are going back to Florida," I tell Gabriel. "She won't go," he says. There is confidence in his voice. A smile on his face. "She loves me too much. She always says, 'Marry me or I'll move back to Florida,' but she never goes."

Never have I hated him more. I refuse to hold his hand.

As we walk into her apartment, it seems Lola is really moving back to Florida. There are boxes and suitcases. The landlord is showing the apartment to some new tenants. Robert is kicking the wall. Lola is about to take him to an exorcist who lives down the block. There is no Christmas tree. I see her underwear on the couch. Empty glasses on the coffee table. Gabriel's face is pale. He speaks to Lola. Words I don't understand, but she is in a hurry. She must take Robert to the exorcist. We must leave.

He and I walk out of the apartment building. I am happy she is moving. I feel I have won a terrible war. Peace is possible now. He looks tired. Defeated. A nearby shopping center is playing Christmas carols on its loudspeaker system and the sound travels down the block to us. "My parents died on Christmas Day, thirty-five years ago," he says. We walk toward Division Street where we will wait for the westbound bus to carry us back home to Eva and Aunt Clara. Aunt Clara will be waiting for us, for him. Darkness is gathering. He has bought me a hat and mittens and I am warm. But the wind is blowing cold and his head and hands are bare. He draws his old leather jacket around his shoulders, its collar up to his ears. He buries his hands into either pocket, where I imagine him feeling in one a plastic egg, in the other a lifeless duck. Then somehow I know for sure magic does not always work. It does not come from God. It does not come from the devil, but from the slight movements of raw and human hands.

Mimosa

Carol Anshaw

The usually hushed gallery rings and lights up like the inside of a pinball machine. The carpenters are here with clattering scaffolds and thwanging hammers. Three people from Graphic Design are adhering small, impeccably correct title cards next to the canvases. There are also two guys the museum hires as lighting consultants. They bring with them more scaffolding from which they dangle and toss around cables thick as Amazon snakes.

In the midst of this, Renata is trying to sound utterly sincere as she speaks to Steve Palm, the artist whose canvasses are the subject of all this hyperactivity. He is unhappy, silent and broody.

"We can rehang the entire show, if necessary," Renata says, putting a hand lightly on his forearm. "Rehanging is not a problem." It would actually be a huge problem, and he knows this. They both know rehanging is not an option. She goes on anyway—"What's important is that *you* feel good about everything"—then waits for whatever mechanisms Steve Palm will have to go through to get back to okay. Sometimes her job irises down to just this, a detached kind of waiting for others to come around to her point of view.

Renata finds a moment to sneak back to hide in her office. "Any calls?" she asks Joan. Joan wears black clothing and powdery white Kabuki-like make-up, and has a diamond stud in the pierced side of her nose. Renata hired her for these affectations, thinking they might indicate someone more interesting than the cardiganed secretaries the museum personnel office has a seemingly endless supply of. Joan, though, has turned out to be cardiganed within. She has a life which revolves around a computer programmer husband and their weekends spent with puzzle maps and thermoses of coffee, driving around the suburbs of Chicago in auto gymkhanas.

Joan holds out a ruffle of pink While You Were Out slips. Renata takes these and sees one is from Kimberly, and her spirits buoy. After the phone number, Joan has written "Sounded like she was calling from bowling alley."

Renata closes the door, sits down at her desk, slips her shoes off onto the carpet and dials the number, which is not a bowling alley, but the shipping department of a small plant that makes trophies and metal plaques. Kimberly heads up this department. She loves her job.

"Yeah?" a guy answers and when Renata has asked for Kimberly, yells (without moving the receiver away from his mouth) "Kimberleeeeee!" And then there is the sound of the dropped receiver clattering again and again against the wall. Renata reads half the catalog

on a ceramics show before Kimberly rescues the
receiver at the other end.

"Yeah?"

"It's me," Renata says.

"Oh. Well, listen. I can't make it tonight. My
brother's coming over with his wife and their new
baby."

"Maybe you could come by later. After they've left."

"Maybe." Kimberly doesn't like to commit to assig-
nations, or keep them once she has, or show up on
time when she has decided she will show up at all.
Renata knows enough not to pressure, and so just
accepts this change in plans, and hangs up.

And is astonished and thrilled when—hours after
she has gone to bed and fallen into a racy, surface
sleep—she awakes to the sound of a key in the lock.
She pretends to be unwakened. She doesn't really
want to talk to Kimberly, doesn't want the light
switched on for a showing of pictures of the new
nephew, or the suggestion that they get up and make
sundaes. (Kimberly is a pageant of impulsive gestures.)
If she keeps her eyes closed and her breathing even,
she will hear clothes falling and feel sheets parting,
and get the Kimberly she wants, naked and needy.

They met several weeks ago at a bar. It was late.
Renata had gone to two gallery openings, then dinner
with two ancient married pairs of collectors. A truly
deadly evening.

Afterward, at the bar, she watched Kimberly dance
with a big-hair and lipstick girl about her age. That is,
about Kimberly's age, which is nineteen, as opposed to
Renata's, which is forty-one. That night Kimberly was
in leather, her hair gelled back. She looked like Garbo

coming out of the sea. Renata caught her between dances, asked if she could buy her a drink.

"A mimosa," Kimberly said. Something in the way she said this made it clear she had given thought to her drink, to having one.

The drink didn't establish any connection, though. Kimberly went back to dancing, this time with someone tall and thin and wearing beat-up khakis and a white T-shirt, a camp counselor look Renata knows stops the hearts of many women, but which does nothing for her. It is only girls like Kimberly who perform a sort of sexual photosynthesis around Renata, leaving her suddenly without enough air available for breathing.

Kimberly seemed to know everyone in the bar, as if tonight were a party to which she had invited them all. It was only after last call that she gave any indication she was aware of Renata's presence.

"We could talk. Or something. We could go to your place," she said. "I live too far for one thing."

The other thing, which Renata didn't find out until a bit later, is that Kimberly still lives at home. Now when Renata calls, she leaves messages, either with Kimberly's mother, or with an answering machine that features the voice of Kimberly's father and the barking of the family dog.

The night of the opening of Steve Palm's show, Renata is in the staff ladies room, fluffing up. She asks Joan, "Do you think this dress is too conservative?"

"The hickey undercuts it," Joan says, tapping a spot on Renata's neck, just below and behind her ear, then lends her some concealer.

Renata supposes Joan, like everyone else at the museum, thinks she goes with Greg Berger, a straight-looking gay collage maker who offers Renata protective coloration in exchange for the opportunity to cozy up to people who might be helpful to his career.

After the opening, to which Greg has come as Renata's escort, she drops him at the apartment of someone new he's seeing, then drives by the bar where she met Kimberly. She does this most nights. If she doesn't see Kimberly's car, she goes by two other bars, then out to the edge of the city where Kimberly lives— a low-to-the-ground yellow brick house, the inside of which is limitedly observable through a picture window framing the huge chrome base of a table lamp, the backs of two arm chairs. The driveway handles a revolving population of cars, one of which is Kimberly's black CRX, which takes a $300 nip out of her monthly paycheck, and is one of her expressed major reasons for still living at home, where her parents charge her only $25 a month rent for her room. Renata has guessed (perhaps incorrectly) which window in the house is this room. If the CRX is in the drive, Renata cuts the engine and sits watching for a while—the house, the CRX, the darkened window— before making the long drive home, where she can rest knowing Kimberly is not out, riling up the night.

Tonight, though, the CRX is in the parking lot of the bar where Renata met Kimberly. She can't just go in and assume that Kimberly will be happy to see her. Kimberly enjoys impulsive gestures only when they are hers. Everyone else should be the rising and setting of the sun, the phases of the moon, the progression of seasons—a calculable backdrop against which Kimberly can provide the weather.

Renata pulls into the lot and parks at the far end. She is prepared to wait until the bar closes, but within the hour Kimberly steps out, jaunty on her pins, an astronaut emerging from some chamber that has been distorting gravity, subverting balance. She is holding onto the arm of the person who has won the Kimberly prize tonight. Renata barely registers this woman, who exists only in that she is occupying the space immediately adjacent to Kimberly, which precludes Renata from occupying this space herself. The dilemma reduces itself to one of emotional physics.

She doesn't need to follow this vignette any further, but does anyway, tailing the car they get into—one of those jeepy boxes set high on oversize tires—a few miles to a neighborhood with next to no parking, where Renata sits in the dark of her car, watching Kimberly and her new friend walk into one entrance of a courtyard building. Lights come on briefly in a third-floor apartment, then go off.

For a year and a half, Renata saw a capable therapist who worked hard to help her tear loose from the relentless, exhausting necessity to be in love with one after another Kimberly. And together, she and the therapist were successful. For two years following the therapy, Renata was not prey to any futile attractions. The problem was, she wasn't prey to any attractions at all. Deprived of her obsession, no other more regular tropisms then became available to her.

"My parents want to meet you," Kimberly says one afternoon about a week later when she is painting Renata's toenails, having talked her into staying home from work. Renata, in turn, called the metal shop, pretending to be Kimberly's mother with news of her daughter's stomach flu.

"Oh," Renata says. "Sure." She tried not to convey any emotion along with these words. Within, she is thrilled at the invitation, even as she is appalled at the idea of going through with it. Kimberly is one of the new breed of babydykes—out to her family practically since puberty (while Renata's relatives are still hoping she meets Mr. Right). And so there is no cover connection to pretend to. She can't come in as Kimberly's French tutor or life drawing instructor. Renata wonders exactly how Kimberly *has* described her, what word she used to designate Renata's position in her life. Having been brought up in conversation to Kimberly's parents gives credence to Renata's pinpoint focus. It means she has a place in the small universe of her obsession.

"Do you have Nintendo?" Kimberly says, out of bed and poking around in the videotapes stacked in the bottom of the TV stand.

"No," Renata says. "I don't have anything. I don't even have cable."

"You should," Kimberly says. "When you need TV, you need enough of it. Cable gives you enough."

She's restless, Renata sees. On the near edge of boredom, a brink Renata does not want to let her slide over.

"Bring me some ice cubes from the refrigerator, will you?" Renata says.

"What for?"

"Crush them down a bit. I'll need little pieces."

Kimberly does as she's told. She's surprisingly obedient for someone so ruthless and willful.

When she is back, Renata gives her permission. "You can take those off," she says, tugging at a bit of elastic, as she puts shards of ice into her mouth, takes another between her fingertips, and begins.

"It's always nice to meet Kimberly's friends," her father says, offering a hand, and standing with the temporary stoop of someone just out of a recliner. It's his hair that makes a strong first impression; it's thick and bristly and randomly combed, like a young Kennedy's.

"Mr. Lazar," Renata says; she hasn't been given a first name.

Kimberly's mother doesn't let this particular awkwardness happen. She dusts Renata into the living room with small, fanning motions of her hands as she says, "Call me Nikki. We're not much for standing on ceremony here."

Renata sees in an instant what she hadn't predicted, also now sees she could have only *not* predicted it by propping up a lead sheet of denial—that these two people are younger than she is. Only by a couple of years, but still.

"Kim has told us so much about you," Nikki says, sitting down, then jumping up again to offer corn chips and guacamole. She is health club thin, her limbs exposed by the rolled-up sleeves of her "JUST DO IT" T-shirt, her black spandex tights.

Mr. Lazar is bringing in a bottle of wine. In the other hand, he has his fingers laced between the stems of wine glasses. Renata has no idea what this "so much" about her has been composed of, and so has no clear response available. She tries smiling as though all the information preceding her has been fascinating and complimentary. She feels suddenly overwhelmingly old. She feels her hair going white, then yellow. Her gums receding, her cheeks lapsing into wattles. Like an unsuccessful escapee from Shangri-la. Like the aging admirer in "Death in Venice." And of course like Humbert Humbert.

✦ ✦ ✦

The conversation doesn't stall out so much as it never really reaches lift-off. The Lazars are undergoing the trauma of kitchen renovation and Renata contributes her own handful of horror stories on the experience. Which only seems to worsen the situation. The more common ground they find, the more ludicrous it seems that Renata should be sitting across the living room from them, their daughter sitting on the floor at her feet. The going gets particularly rough when Nikki asks Renata if she has any children herself.

Kimberly is the only one who seems to be at ease. She both sits at Renata's feet and also accepts a small plate filled with tortilla chips her mother has pre-dipped in guacamole for her daughter, and in neither position indicates the slightest discomfort.

Renata, on the other hand, listens to Mr. Lazar explain his business, which is the moving of items both heavy and fragile—grand pianos, alabaster urns and such. In this context he has met a few art collectors and runs their names past Renata who, in not recognizing them, feels like a prospective employee unable to provide references. She has, she realizes too late, only after she has drawn blood, been gnawing at her cuticles, a habit she broke in college. She also finds a glob of guacamole on the knee of her white linen pants.

"You should get that off," Kimberly says in an over-urgent tone, as though something has happened which will require a tourniquet, the raising of feet above the victim's head. "I'll show you where the john is. Get you a washcloth."

She takes Renata down a narrow hall, their footfalls absorbed by a thick, pale blue cushion of carpet. When they reach the bathroom at the end, Kimberly gives Renata a light shove inside, then follows and pushes the door shut behind them with her back. She is slightly taller than Renata, also bigger boned. And so she can create the physical impression that she is swooping Renata up into her arms.

Renata closes her eyes as she feels first the lips, then the teeth at her neck. It is absurdly and regrettably in moments such as these that Renata feels her most authentic self. Which means the rest of everything must be shaped to the absurd contours of this fascination.

There is a meeting of all the museum's curators and department heads. State funding has been cut again, which means positions will also be trimmed, along with salaries. Everyone has been expecting this; it's no surprise. But now they can all see the axe above them, beginning its fall.

Enid, the museum director's secretary, scuttles in through a side door of the boardroom. "I'm sorry," she says in her rangy Australian accent, then signals to Renata that she should step outside.

Renata tries to imagine what could have happened, what terrible news awaits on the other side of the door, what could have persuaded Enid, who takes her job as seriously as a sentry in a turret, to interrupt this uninterruptible meeting. Renata imagines some nameless piece of bad news, sees herself crumpling onto a chair, being instructed by Enid to put her head down between her knees.

"It's your mum," is what Enid actually says, and Renata's heart slips inside her. Her mother is seventy-four and has high blood pressure. Renata just talked with her two days earlier, though, and she sounded fine. "There's been an accident, I'm afraid. She was hit. By a cement truck apparently. Someone called from the hospital. A nurse in the emergency room. Frightfully noisy. I couldn't really hear all the details."

Renata doesn't have to look down at the slip of paper Enid is handing her. She already knows what number will be written there. For months to come she will have to make up reports of her mother's progress, her recuperation, to Enid and the others who will be solicitous.

Moments later, behind the closed door of her office, she shouts into the receiver, into the background din, "What? What is it?"

There's a long pause, filled in with racket, then finally, "I just don't like it when I can't get you. They say you're in a meeting. I mean, what does that really *mean?*"

Renata explains that occasionally—in this case, for instance—it means she is actually in a meeting.

"Well, I don't like it, though. Sometimes I need to get hold of you."

"Like now," Renata guesses, but she is wrong.

"No. This time is just a test. Like for the emergency broadcasting system. This time there's only a tone." Kimberly imitates the tone. It's amazing how long she is able to hold it without taking a breath.

In Kerry's Cab

Diane Williams

Eyelids weighted with a need for sleep and heart weary with what-might-have-been, Kerry pulled over to pick up the young woman flagging her as she turned the cab onto Belmont. The rear door on the passenger side opened, and Kerry looked up at the rearview mirror and into a freckled, cinnamon-colored face, a sister's face, with an "X" cap shrouding its eyes. The fare climbed in, slammed the door, and slumped against the back seat. Kerry scanned her quickly and settled again in her own seat as she gripped the steering wheel.

"Are you going my way?" The fare's buttery voice massaged the back of Kerry's neck.

"That depends on how far you're going." Kerry smiled into the mirror, but she could not brush away that feeling, that *something* buzzing around her like an insect.

Kerry had felt that *something* encircling her as she got into her cab that night. This *something* was palpa-

ble, clinging to every bit of bare skin—face, ungloved
hands—in the before-dawn chill. But she had wanted
to drive anyway, to get out of the apartment, to get
away from what Bridget had branded The Truth.
Puffing a filterless cigarette, Kerry had slid behind the
wheel and let her new lover's words flash through her
mind. She had heard them before, screaming from different mouths—lipsticked mouths; hard-as-stone
mouths; white, well-meaning mouths; mouths black
and hungry like her own—it did not matter. Always
the melody was the same:

"Why can't you just let me love you, Kerry?"

"Don't ask me that. I do love you."

"That's not what I said."

"That's what I heard."

"Because you hear what you want."

"I didn't come here for this."

"Why did you come here?"

Kerry had answered with only a shrug and a
slammed door. Then she had done what she always
did when she was puzzled: sit in her white and red
cab, smoking, idling the engine, watching people, now
watching the darkness fight into light.

In spite of the feeling that she should just go back
to Bridget's tiny apartment and huge embrace, she had
pulled away from the curb and left Bridget's brown-
stone in the rearview.

She had driven north, up Halsted, toward Belmont,
hoping to catch someone tumbling out of a Chicago
bar after a long Saturday night. It had been drier,
warmer, more springlike that week, and people had
begun to flood the streets again. Good for business.
What else was there if there was no business, no work?

Now she had business, validation, a passenger who
did not seem unfriendly or drunk, just young and
cloaked in trends: the cap, the jacket with some sports
team's logo—Magic, it said—the baggy jeans, the high

tops. *That could be me ten years ago*, Kerry thought; *I hope she doesn't want to go somewhere I don't want to go tonight.* Normally she would take fares almost anywhere they wanted to go, but not now, not with her body sagging and her mind cloudy.

"Pardon the cliche, but where to, mac?"

"Western and Milwaukee," the fare said.

"No problem." Kerry cranked down the meter flag and eased into traffic, what little there seemed to be at five in the blessed a.m. She adjusted the rearview to keep her fare in full sight. The fare pulled out a pack of slender, beige cigarettes.

"Can I smoke in this vehicle, or does the city ordinance cover cabs too, ba-bee?"

The word *baby* moved like an ice cube down Kerry's spine, but she only glanced at the woman in the rearview and said, "Feel free."

The lit cigarette filled the cab with the scent of burning something—grass, maybe even lettuce—and Kerry realized that her *cooooool* passenger smoked French cigarettes. She laughed softly.

"What's so funny—" the fare looked over the front seat at Kerry's cab-license picture "—Kerry Marie Green?"

"A memory, that's all." Kerry felt that *something* creeping up from someplace in the pit of her stomach, and she tightened her grip on the wheel.

"If it's funny, I'd like to hear it."

"No, it's not particularly funny. It's just about a girl who was seventeen and liked to smoke foreign cigarettes."

"Do you mean me?"

"No—I mean me."

The fare flicked her ashes onto the floor. "These things cost money, you know, and they taste like burning bushes, but it's the idea of the thing. Sometimes I do things just because I like the idea of them. Don't you do things like that?"

Kerry actually tried to ponder that question, but her mind was wrapped in gauze: too much of what her father would have called *woman trouble* and too little sleep.

"No," she finally said, "I don't."

"That's really too bad. Really."

Kerry shrugged.

While the fare finished that cigarette and stubbed it out in the little metal ashtray in the arm of the car door, Kerry negotiated the cab to Western and Milwaukee.

"Pull over here, ba-bee."

Kerry pulled over a block from the all-night White Castle, and that *something* settled on her chest.

"That'll be four-twenty."

In that instant between stopping the meter and turning to face her fare, Kerry found, the fare had drawn a gun, an indelicate .38, from the pocket of that Magic jacket, and pressed the cold end of the barrel against Kerry's temple.

"I want a free ride, ba-bee, and all of your cash, or this will be your last fare."

Kerry had been driving for over a year. Shouldn't she have listened to that thing inside? Shouldn't she have thought or felt or done something differently? What now did she have to do besides think that, Christ, she was going to die?

Yes, she wished she could have said to someone besides this brand-new bandit, it was true: someone who was unfortunate enough to have time to think before the impact of death did see instances of her life before the final blow. Things began to tumble out of Kerry, out of order, falling like playing cards being flipped randomly into a fedora.

✦ ✦ ✦

She is sitting in this cab, this Death Star 2000, for
the first time. It begins to rain, drops tattooing the
windshield, the wipers creating their own rhythms
against the squawk of the radio. She lights a cigarette
at a traffic stop, and beyond the flame of her Dad's
old butane, she sees something oozing from the top of
the windshield. It begins to seep from the corners
where glass meets roof, and it is pink and almost
transparent in the rain, and she thinks that she is in
a horror movie, *The Amityville Horror* or that one
where Jack Nicholson chases Shelley Duvall around
an old inn with an ax in his hands, one of those
movies where stuff—red, movie-made stuff that she
is supposed to believe is blood—pours from walls,
gushes down stairs, floods the street. She won't
touch it.

She cruises back to the garage, the wipers spreading
this pinkness across the windshield, her rose-colored
windshield.

The dispatcher and the mechanic and two other
drivers huddle around the cab like doctors around a
patient on an operating table, all of them glaring at
the *stuff* and then at each other.

"So, Hector," she says to the mechanic, "what is
this stuff that looks like movie blood?"

Hector chews his toothpick; then he looks into her
eyes.

"It's blood."

"Excuse me?" Something tastes bad at the back of
her throat. "That's not funny."

Hector scratches the thick black hair beneath his
white-and-black Sox cap. "I ain't laughing. It's blood."

Frank, the dispatcher, nods at her and walks over to
put an arm around her shoulder. His white-shirted
stomach melts over his belt like a large marshmallow.

He guides her away from the cab as Hector hoses the windshield. He whispers to her about this cab and the driver who used to drive it and the robbery and the bullet that shattered his American dream and splattered the windshield's inside with blood and brain and bone.

"We thought we had hosed it all out, and we let the cab sit for awhile." Frank tightens his grip on her shoulder. "Don't worry. It'll be okay."

No, it won't be okay—not when people splatter you for a wad of dollar bills. But the next day she takes the Death Star 2000 out for a run anyway, and it belongs to her.

✦ ✦ ✦

Blood. Brain. Bone. Kerry tried to remember how to breathe. A few intelligible words slipped out between gasps.

"I . . . don't . . . have . . . money . . ."

"C'mon, ba-bee." The bandit settled back against the door, both hands squeezing the gun. She was so young, so calm. "You know you've got some money, Kerry Marie."

"You're getting personal here." Kerry did not take her gaze from the barrel or her mind from the thought that today Hector would make a special trip down to the garage to chew his toothpicks and hose off the windshield. She was going to die for four-twenty. "What's your name?"

"Oprah." The freckled face smiled at her, teeth like a beacon in the dimness of the back seat. The cab idled yards from a street lamp, and the bandit's eyes were shadows. "Winfrey."

"Pleased to meet you, but I don't have any money, Oprah."

"You're lying, ba-bee, and I don't know why." The voice flowed still like butter.

"I'm not lying." Kerry felt beads of sweat forming on her forehead, her upper lip. Her down vest was much too warm. Images of Bridget flickered through her head. "Why would I lie to you?"

"You tell me, Kerry Marie." The bandit lit another French cigarette, and acrid smoke haloed her "X" cap. So cool.

They sit in the back row of the Three Penny Cinema, watching *Hearts of Darkness*, amazed at how big this movie is. Excess—beautiful excess—238 days of excess. Brando is bloated and out of dialogue. Bridget's leg is draped across Kerry's. They are on their free popcorn refill in spite of the slaughtered caribou staggering across the screen. It is a religion, Eleanor Coppola narrates. Blood is the reddest red in the universe, Bridget says softly, her breath tickling Kerry's face. Redder than Mars. Kerry agrees. Her hand wanders across the miracle of Bridget's thigh. The Coke is icy. The chocolate bar is dark, thick. Martin Sheen has broken down and is wailing, bloody and naked, in his hotel room. She wants to kiss Bridget.

Later, in Bridget's apartment, they sip tea—Red Zinger—and listen to Sade and pretend they are Alice B. Toklas and Gertrude Stein. Kerry feels Bridget's gaze on her body. Smiling, beckoning with the curve of her mouth. Kerry does not remember moving, but she is now on her knees in front of Bridget, whose thighs are bare beneath the summer cotton of her dress. Kerry is kissing Bridget's mouth, stroking her legs, nibbling at her breasts beneath the cotton violets. Bridget's fingers caress Kerry's back. Movie posters make the apartment a theater. They are surrounded by Gable and Garbo, Bogart and Bacall, King Kong and the Wizard of Oz, and Bridget's giggle on her neck is all the permission Kerry needs.

Kerry closed her eyes tightly, yet she could see Bridget's face in ecstasy, the mouth crumpled in laughter, the eyes wide and consuming. She swallowed, yet she could feel the words *I'm sorry* forming in her throat, choking her.

Kerry had come so far from a lover's comfort, those moments when no voices told her none of that was real, none of that stuff was important. Only work and the money made mattered. Now *Money Made* would be engraved on her tombstone; it would be all she would have as an apology.

Kerry watched the bandit breathing, still, silent too long, her jacket rising and falling slowly in the shadows of the back seat. Each word spoken meant another second when the bandit's finger did not squeeze that trigger.

"I just started." Kerry spoke as calmly as she could. "Is this the early-early shift or the late-late shift?"

"Both."

"Give me what you got. Be careful, girlfriend."

Kerry searched her pockets, turning them inside out, picking out single dollar bills like lint and tossing them into the back seat. The rest of the money was with Bridget as it usually was, in a coffee can on a shelf, waiting for a proper counting.

"I *am* a girlfriend, Oprah." Oprah. Too cool, too impudent. "You shouldn't do this to a sister."

"I'm an only child, Kerry Marie."

"But I've got a wife and children." Kerry shook her head at her own folly, her own desperation for another godawful moment.

The bandit smiled. "Oh? Is that why you work Broadway?"

At her father's funeral she stands away from the crowd of mourners. *Don't let nobody get too close.* She is twenty, and already she knows hypocrisy is a cloak worn at times like this. Her mother, who must be wiping away tears of relief, is sustaining her grandmother, who has no idea what her perfect son was really like after he took off his black usher's suit on Sunday afternoons. Kerry has learned her lessons well. *It's money*, he would tell her brothers and her. *It's the business*, he would say between his nightcaps, his after-work unwinders, his weekend socializers. Glass after glass. Bottle after bottle. The children would concentrate on each word, as if spoken by a man who embraced sobriety and kindness. They would soak up his every edict rather than let their minds wander and their eyes betray them. That would bring a harsh word followed by a heavy hand. Mother had long ago stopped defending them, for they took what she would have gotten. Instead she stocked the pantry with his favorite whisky, his expensive brandy.

"It's only the work," she hears now in her father's gruffness. "Don't drive a cab for somebody else. Buy your own cab. Didn't I teach you anything? It's just the money, the damned dollar. I didn't have anything, worked my tired black ass off so you could have something. . . . No, not for somebody else . . . the damned dollar. . . ."

She stands away from everyone, hoping that she can hold all of these lessons inside as the preacher blesses "this fine brother." She leans against a tree, her stomach churning. The lessons go on.

"Don't let nobody get too close. They get your heart, they'll get your brain. They get your brain, they'll get your soul. Mark my words."

Kerry does mark his words, all of them, day by day, year by year.

Kerry had not forgotten, and now she would die with everyone who loved her at arm's length, her heart and soul tucked away safely.

"Don't do this, sister."

Kerry dropped the word *sister* between the bandit and herself like a pane of bullet-proof glass, the kind that her company was too—what did they call it?—*cost conscious* to put in their cabs. Hosing a windshield was certainly more cost effective. She wiped the flannel of a sleeve across her upper lip.

The bandit had snatched up the money and now stuffed it into her jacket.

"I told you I'm an only child, an orphan, too."

"So, you're robbing me because you like the idea or because you need the money?"

"Money makes the world go, Kerry Marie."

The bandit aimed the gun at Kerry's forehead, and Kerry said goodbye—to everyone, their names and pictures spilling through her mind the way she imagined she would spill onto the front seat.

Click. Blood.

Click. Brain.

Click. Bone.

Kerry opened her eyes, amazed that nothing—not even lightning—had struck her.

"This must be your lucky day, sis-tuh." The bandit climbed out of the back seat. "I played Russian Rou-

lette, and you won. Congratulations." She slammed
the door and disappeared down the street, through the
White Castle parking lot, the gun snug in the jacket.
No one seemed to stir anywhere.

Kerry waited. No driving, no screaming, no radio
calling—for the moment she could simply sit and re-
shuffle the cards of her life into an acceptable deck:
The Truth yet Not The Truth.

Service

June Rachuy Brindel

The red light on the dashboard had flashed some
miles back. Out of gas. The expressway was deserted.
Thick fog coming down fast. She kept driving, hoping
for an exit before the tank emptied completely. At last
she saw one, with the lights of a service station just beyond. She coughed up to a pump and died.

As soon as the motor went off, the cold settled
around her neck like a muffler. An attendant hove
into the window on her left, haloed by the steam of
his breath. She lowered the glass a timid inch. "Fill it
up." She fumbled in her purse. He squinted through
the haze. Shook his head. And walked away.

The window frosted over at once. Had the warmth
in the car spouted out through the crack? She closed
the window, snapped shut her purse and waited. Another car had pulled in on the other side of the pump,
the misty outlines of it glowing through the frost. In
the rearview mirror she could see the attendant rush-
ing past to the other driver's window. A thick cloud of

confidential laughter floated over the hood. "Goddamn," she whispered resentfully. She rubbed a hole
in the frost, noticed a star on the side of the other car
and relented. Cops. An obligation. Maybe an emergency? She hauled up a philosophic resignation, pulled
off her glove and lit a cigarette.

The smoke seemed heavier than usual. It clung to
the windshield like a wraith. She leaned over to open
the window on the passenger side and a sharp wind
scythed in before she could close it again, sweeping
out the smoke but chilling her spine. At this, the fog
suddenly lifted and the frost died on the pane. The
police car drove silently away and the attendant returned. He was talking to her through the glass,
but the sound of the wind was so loud that she
couldn't hear what he was saying. She struggled with
the window, but it stuck now as though frozen. By the
time she had it open, the attendant had gone back
into the office. The wind shrieked through the car as
if the sides had disappeared. She clenched the glowing
cigarette in fierce teeth and strained against the window crank until her fingernails broke. And then suddenly, without effort, the window closed. She sank
back exhausted.

After a while she opened her eyes. The attendant
was moving back and forth behind the cans of oil
displayed in the window, as if on urgent business,
though there seemed to be no one else around. A
prior order, perhaps, that had to be filled at the cost
of keeping a paying customer waiting? A police order?
Perhaps they were coming back at any moment to
pick up something they needed in a hurry. Oil? The
cans rested imperturbably along the bottom frame of
the window, while the attendant continued to rush
from office to garage and back, his movements hectic,
even feverish. She could not make out their purpose.
He held his hands shoulder high, and exactly parallel

as if carrying something about two feet wide. But no object could be seen. Perhaps it was transparent.

Her cigarette had burned down. She decided against opening the window again and stubbed it out in the overfilled tray, scattering ash in a fine spray up against her glasses. When she had wiped them clean again, the attendant had disappeared from sight.

Her windows were now sealed on both sides, but the wind found ways to enter. She reached into the back seat for the woolen scarf she had thrown off some time before and draped it across her shoulders. It was odd that the attendant had not returned to fill her tank. She wondered what he had said. Perhaps he had been left alone unexpectedly (in a station this size they would surely have more than one attendant) and on a miserable night (it had begun to snow) with who knows what personal traumas (wives with miscarriages, children with appendectomies). In the warmth of the scarf, she could begin to sympathize with the problems of gas station attendants on frigid nights in lonely posts on interminable expressways.

She had been staring so intently at the office window that the attendant's sudden presence at her left cheek startled her and her heart began the erratic leap-flop-gap-flop that had interested the doctor in the last town. She wrestled frantically with the window crank and lowered it just in time to hear, "Can't take care of you," before he disappeared again in a swirl of snow. Well, then. He was out of gas. And in a growing blizzard. (The snow had increased violently.) Perhaps delivery trucks were stalled in snowbanks somewhere along the line, though she had seen none on the expressway. Or was it another gas shortage? A boycott she had not heard about? A sense of shared adventure made her feel almost fond of the attendant. She decided to brave the wind and go into the office. Very likely he would explain everything. At any rate, it would be warm.

But as she touched the door handle, the snow stopped and a green station wagon filled with laughing children pulled up on the other side of the pump. Immediately the attendant appeared, hood thrown back, jacket open. He was running toward the station wagon, laughing as he went and lithe as an athlete. He veered sharply around her car, placed one hand on the hood of the station wagon, and leaped several feet into the air to the applause and merriment of the children. Even the driver, who looked to be scarcely more than a child himself, guffawed in an exaggerated way, disproportionate to the occasion unless some in-joke were involved. There was a good deal of uproarious interchange which the wind carried off even though she lowered the window to listen. And then the attendant (she saw now how young he was) opened the gas tank of the station wagon with a theatrical flourish and filled it to the brim and over, in a careless abandon which provoked a renewal of laughter from the children. At which the attendant retreated to ten feet behind the wagon, rushed forward, leaped up on the back window, ran over the top, and sprang off the hood into the air, tumbling into bushes at the far end of the concrete. All the children shrieked in delight, the driver shouted, the station wagon roared extravagantly and sped away.

She slammed the door of the car and stalked after the retreating attendant. An outrage. He hadn't even charged them for the gas. Somebody higher up ought to know about that. A sudden wind snatched the office door out of her hand and crashed it shut after her, almost splintering the glass. There was no one in the office though she heard the sound of something heavy being pushed in the garage area. Then there was a clatter and the grind of a hydraulic lift ascending, and several voices shouting incomprehensible jargon back and forth through echoing metal. So he was not even alone!

She started through a door into the garage, but was blocked at once by a huge grease-covered man.

"Can't go in there, lady," he mumbled.

"I would like some service," she said stiffly.

The hulk grunted. Even his lips were muscular, tough. He filled the doorway like a stopper. "You, Mike!" he stared past her head.

Behind her, at the desk (how had he got there?) sat the first attendant, as if materializing on call. His face was still merry, but his voice was apologetic. "We can't take care of you." He smiled.

She was bewildered. A bell rang. Mike vaulted over the desk and dashed out to the pumps. "Just a minute," she said. Doors closed in her face.

It was very dark now and the service area was lit by only a single lamp above each pump. As she watched Mike filling a white Mercury Cougar, a black Porsche flashed in and pulled up right behind her ancient Chevy, honking loudly. She hurried out, feeling the wind snake in under her coat. The Cougar roared away and another slithered into its place.

"Can you help me now?" she asked, as the Porsche honked. Mike's smile was angelic but he didn't seem to hear her. She tried again. The Porsche backed up with a screech and pulled over to a pump she hadn't noticed before. Other attendants were running out to the service area now. And many cars, whipping in and out, barely pausing to be filled. Only hers sat still. Constantly cars pulled up behind it, blasted impatiently, then backed up and found another pump. Mike had disappeared. She grabbed at one of the other attendants as he ran toward the office, but the blue sleeve brushed past her numb fingers. Suddenly, she noticed that the huge greasy man from the garage had come out and was pushing her car to the side.

She ran over to him and said, "Stop." He kept on pushing, steering with one hand. "Goddamn crate's blocking traffic," he muttered. A blue Mercedes snorted into her place.

"I don't understand!" she shouted, standing frozen in the path of a red MG. "Why can't I have some service?"

The huge greasy man jammed her car up against the bushes lining the service area and vanished again into the garage.

"Mike!" she screamed.

At once he appeared beside her, smiling politely. "We don't have your kind of gas."

"But I can't go on without it." The tears on her eyelashes were beginning to freeze.

"I know." His voice was full of sympathy, but he walked away. She sprinted after him. "Excuse me," she cried. A gold Buick swept by, almost crunching her toes. "I've never had this trouble before," she told a red-headed attendant. He clicked his tongue and disappeared behind a purple Mazda. Across the lot she saw Mike getting into a battered truck. He met her eyes briefly, smiled, waved and raced out onto the expressway.

The cold came down then as if the air had congealed. Her legs felt like stilts as she walked to the office. No one was at the desk, but several men huddled around a hissing heater. One of them moved over to make room for her, a brownish man with features blurred as if the paint might have run on his portrait. "I don't know what to do," she confided as her fingers straightened in the warmth. He shook his head. "You could ride with me, but I'm going in the other direction." The man beside him let out a long breath.

"Talk to the boss, why doncha?" It was a voice that struggled out through layers of phlegm. It came from behind her. Her hands froze again when she turned.

He was sitting on the desk top, his legs dangling
unevenly, one at least a foot longer than the other.
His face was red and blue in blotches and a mon-
strous wen swelled from his left temple. "He's a
sonofabitch," he rattled.

"Where is he?"

"Who? Harve?"

"The boss."

"That's Harve. He's a sonofabitch."

"Where is he?"

His hand paused to scratch the wen and traveled on
in a vague gesture in the direction of the garage. She
could hear muffled clinks and voices. The door sprang
open at her touch and again the huge grease covered
man filled the frame. "I want to talk to Harve," she
said. This time he backed away.

Only two men were in the garage, at opposite
ends of a car up on a rack. They talked constantly.
"Torquom pratio ratio," one shouted. "Shaft aft,"
answered the other. The metallic walls made the
words echo back upon themselves. She could understand nothing. She walked close so that they would be
sure to see her and waited for a pause in the conversation. It did not come. She approached the one at the
hood, but as she neared him, he retreated around the
other side of the car. She followed, he kept retreating
until both of them and the other man as well had circled the car three times. The conversation had not
paused.

"Excuse me," she said. No one heard. "Pardon me
me me!" she shrieked. They paid no attention. She
picked up a rod from the floor and banged it loudly
against the machinery for inflating tires. It bent and
flew out of her hands against the outer door, missing
one of the men by inches. He picked up the rod and
looked at her in silence, his arm raised. "I am sorry
about that," she whispered.

The other man was also silent now, looking at her.

"Which one of you is Harve?" Her hands were freezing again. The men didn't move. "I'd like to speak with the manager, is one of you him? He?"

It became strangely silent both inside and out. Suddenly the men threw down their tools with a clang and walked toward her. "Watch your step, lady," said one. "We're just closing up," said the other.

"You see, I'm out of gas, and I can't seem to get any service."

The first man nodded and kept moving. "Harve would be the one you should see." They both walked into the office. She followed. The room was empty. The heater had gone out. The first man came out of the toilet in a huge parka, carrying a set of keys. "Locking up now, lady." He turned a key in the cash register.

"Look here, I want my tank filled up right this minute, you hear?"

"You can wait in the office for Harve, if you want to," said the man.

"I don't understand. I never had any trouble before."

"The heater works pretty good." He locked the doors.

But it was plain to see that the heater was not working at all. Through the bleary window she saw the two garage men driving off in a small pickup. The service area was deserted except for her own car up against the bushes. Only a dim light burned in the office. The cold was pressing in against her on all sides. She examined the heater. It was plugged in, but lifeless.

After some time the bulb went out.

The Man Who Loved Life

Sara Paretsky

Simon Peter Dresser looked down at the long rows of tables. Pride made his heart grow in his chest, pressing against his throat so that he could hardly respond to the bishop sitting on his right. If only his daddy could see him now, bishops deferring to him, politicians courting him and hundreds of people looking up to where he sat at the center of the head table, admiration glowing from their faces.

His daddy had snorted when Simon told him he'd been asked to head the Illinois group. That was in 1975, two years after the baby murderers had persuaded the family haters on the Supreme Court to give women all over America abortion on demand.

Leave politics to the politicians, the old man had said. You got enough to do looking after your own family. Then he died before Simon's picture appeared in *Newsweek*. Died before Simon got the invitation to address the House of Bishops. He'd have seen that Simon truly was a rock, the rock on which a whole nation of Christians was building its hope of bringing morality back to America. Yes, Simon Peter, on this rock I will build my church. His daddy picked him to be the rock because he was the oldest and the younger ones had to obey him just like he had to obey his daddy. But sometimes the old man had his doubts. If only he could have lived to see this night.

Simon's heart started thudding faster and louder as he thought of the praise that lay ahead for him. Although the steak was cut thick and cooked the way he liked it, just a little pink showing, he could hardly taste it for excitement. But he politely handed sour cream to the bishop and glanced at Louise to make sure she was talking to the state representative on her left. He'd tried to impress on her before they left home how important it was to pay attention to the man, how much Simon needed him to carry out his program for Illinois, how she couldn't do her usual trick of staring at her plate all through dinner.

When she saw him looking at her she flushed and put down her fork and blurted something to her dinner partner. Simon shook his head a little, but nothing could really dampen his exultation. And it wasn't fair to her, not really; she wasn't at home with crowds and speeches as he was. She seldom came with him to public events. She didn't like to leave the children, even now that Tommy was eight and could get along without her.

He turned back to the bishop and delivered a short lecture on tactics in response to a comment the prelate had made with the sour cream.

"Of course it's largely a social problem," the bishop said when Simon finished. "The breakdown of the family. Parents unwilling to assume any moral authority. Very few with your kind of family-centered life. But you don't need me to tell you that."

"It's a question of respect," Simon said. "Children don't respect their parents and their parents don't do anything to force them to. It was different when you and I were boys. You take my old man. You said 'yessir' when you spoke to him or he made sure you never forgot a second time."

The bishop smiled in polite agreement and told a long tale about the demoralized state of modern seminary training. Simon took another roll and explained that his daddy had been tough. Tough, but fair. He'd sometimes felt hurt when he was little, but now he thanked God he had a father like that, one who knew right from wrong and wouldn't put up with any crap. Nossir, you thought you were being slick, putting one over the old man, but he was always a jump ahead of you. Had a hand as strong as a board. He wasn't afraid to use it, not even when you got to be big as him. Bigger.

The bishop nodded and shared an anecdote about the man he'd first served under as a priest.

Simon pursed his lips and shook his head at the right places. That time he'd gone out drinking with his buddies, he'd been eighteen, getting ready to start at St. Xavier's (stay with the Jesuits, his daddy said; they don't snivel every time some JD comes to them with a hard-luck story). He'd thought he was old enough to do what he wanted on Saturday night.

Don't be a sissy, for Christ's sake. He was pretty sure it was Jimmy who had put it into words, Jimmy who was going into the army along with Bobby Lee Andrews. That was when being a soldier meant something, not like now, when all the soft liberals in Congress encourage kids to burn their own country's flag. So he and Jimmy and Bobby went out with Carl and Joe. One last get-together for the team before they went their separate ways. The other guys were always on him, how he was scared of his old man. They

didn't recognize it was respect, not fear. You respect
the man who's strong enough to know right from
wrong and teach it to you.

But just that one time he couldn't take their hassling
any more. He got weak, soft, caved in and went out
with them. And then two in the morning, giggling
drunk, trying to sneak in through the back door. His
mother had left the back door open. She knew he was
up to something so she snuck down and unlocked it.
She was always soft, always weak, trying to subvert
his daddy's strength. His father made rules and she
tried to break them, but she couldn't. Nossir, not any
more than her children. If she was fifteen dollars shy
in the grocery money his daddy knew: he added all
the bills against her household allowance. Don't tell
me you lost a receipt, Marie, because I sure as hell
don't believe you. Where'd that money go to, anyway?
And she'd snuffle around and cry and try to lie, but
his daddy could always tell.

It was disgusting watching her cry; it made him sick
even to this day when he thought about it. He'd told
Louise that back the first year they were married.
Don't ever cry in front of your children, he warned
her. At least, I'd better not ever hear of you doing it.

"The trouble is," he said to the bishop, "too many
men just are too lazy or too scared to buck all these
libbers and liberals and take on their role as head of
the family. They'd just as soon the government or the
schools or someone did it for them. That's why you
get all these girls going into the abortuaries and letting
someone murder their babies. Their daddies or their
husbands are just too damned—excuse me,
Your Grace—too darned lazy to control them."

The bishop smiled again, as if he was used to hearing people swear and used to hearing them apologize
for it.

Simon's glow of satisfaction extended to his well-run family. None of his five daughters ever talked back to him. None of them had ever even tried, except Sandra. She was the oldest; maybe she thought that gave her special status, but he'd sure as hell beaten that nonsense out of her.

He didn't believe it when she was born. When the nurse came out and told him it was a girl he knew she'd made a mistake, confused him with one of the other men waiting for news. His daddy'd been so disappointed. Disappointed but pleased at the same time: it proved he was a bigger man than Simon would ever be. Then it had taken three more tries before they got their first boy and he was a skinny little runt, took after Louise's family. And then his daddy died before they got their second boy. They named him Tom for his grandpa, and he looked like him, a big, muscly boy, but it was too late; his daddy never saw Simon had finally gotten himself a real little man.

He realized he'd missed the bishop's next remark, but it didn't matter: he'd had the same conversation a hundred times and could respond without thinking. Not like the first time he'd talked to a bishop. Really talked, face to face, not just a handshake after a special service. He'd been so nervous his voice had come out in a little squeak, that high squeak he'd hated because it was how he always ended up sounding if he tried to argue with his daddy. But now he could see the bishops were men just like him, with the same kind of problems running their dioceses he had running his organization. Except now that he was head of the thing for the whole country it was probably more like being pope. Of course he never said any of this to the bishops, but it did give him a little edge over the man on his right. Just a suffragen, an assistant. Maybe twenty parishes under his care. Not like being responsible for the whole country.

The waitress filled Simon's coffee cup. He took cream and sugar from the bishop and used them generously. When he turned to offer them to Louise he saw she'd already been given some by the state representative. She shouldn't use so much sugar; she'd never really gotten her figure back after Tommy was born. But he wasn't going to spoil his big night by worrying about her problems.

As the bishop finished his dessert Simon's heart started its happy thudding once more. The bishop deliberately folded his napkin in threes across the diagonal and put it on the table so it was exactly parallel with his plate. He waited for the master of ceremonies to inform the diners that they would have grace after dinner, then slowly stood and offered the benediction.

Simon fixed a pleased but humble look under his beard. He leaned over to the bishop when he sat down and made a jovial little comment. The bishop nodded and chuckled and everyone on the floor could see that Simon was on equal, maybe even superior terms, with a bishop.

The master of ceremonies told everyone how happy he was they could be here to honor Simon. A staunch fighter for the unborn. . . . Untold thousands of lives saved because of him. . . . Wouldn't rest until babies were safe all over America. . . . Special tribute tonight. . . . But first they'd prepared a slide show: The Fight to Protect the Unborn.

The lights in the ballroom were dimmed and a screen unfolded on the stage behind the head table. Simon and the bishop turned their chairs around so they could see. After a second's hesitation, in which she looked first at Simon, then the state representative, Louise scooted around as well.

Simon had seen portions of the slide show before, sections that were used at fund-raising events and which showed him shaking hands with the President after their historic March for Life at the nation's capital. But they'd put that part together with a series taken at demonstrations and other important events around the country and added a soundtrack. The whole show had been completed in time for tonight's dinner. They'd use it in the future to educate high school students and church groups on how to fight for Life, but it was being unveiled tonight just for him.

Their logo flashed on the screen while solemn but cheerful music played behind it. The dove of the Holy Spirit spreading its wings over the curled form of a helpless fetus. Then his own voice, his well-practiced tenor that he'd spent four years in college studying speech to perfect, to get rid of that shameful squeak. It was a clip from the talk he'd made in Washington, the warm tones vibrating with emotion as he told the gathered hosts that no one in America could be free until every unborn life in America was held sacred.

While they played the speech, pictures flashed on the screen showing the mass of Pro-Life marchers carrying banners, holding up crosses to which they'd nailed cut-outs of murdered babies, all the marchers looking ardently at Simon, some with tears of shared passion in their eyes. Even now, six years later, listening to his own words his throat tightened again with rage felt on behalf of those million-and-a-half babies murdered every year. Hands as big as his father's coming down to choke the life out of them. Even when he'd been eighteen, old enough to go to college, he hadn't been big enough to stand up to the old man, so how could a poor helpless baby in the womb who didn't have any hands at all stand up for itself?

The show went on to display pictures of Pro-Life activists marching outside death camps. Cheers came from the audience when the photo of a fire-bombed death chamber was projected on the screen. They'd have to take that one out when they showed it to the high school students, but it proved that the helpless could gain power if they banded together.

The camera zoomed in close to the face of a girl going into one of the camps as she passed a line of peaceful picketers trying to get her to change her mind. Her face was soft, weak, scared.

Simon's fists clenched in his lap. Something about the girl made him think of his own mother. When his father beat him, her face had that same expression, frightened but withdrawn, a bystander at the torment of her own baby. Don't do it, Thomas, she would beg, tears streaming down her face. He couldn't stand to hear her crying, as if she was the one being punished, and all the candy hearts she gave him later never really soothed him. He never let Louise cry. She'd done it the first time he'd had to give Sandra a whipping for talking back to him. She'd come to him sobbing as if being weak and scared was any way to stop him teaching his children right from wrong. He'd made it real clear she was never to do it again.

Then the girl in the picture was shown changing her mind. The Pro-Life counselor was able to persuade her to put Life above her own selfish desires to control her body. The audience cheered again as the girl walked off with the counselor to a Pro-Life clinic, funded with donations by tens of thousands of little people just like them who cared enough for Life to donate a few dollars every week.

Simon's fists relaxed and his mind wandered off to the remarks he'd make when his turn came. He'd worked on them all week, while flying to Toronto to protest the suspension of a policeman who wouldn't stand guard outside a death camp, while meeting in Springfield with key legislators on a number of bills to protect the unborn. He wanted to sound spontaneous, but authoritative, a leader people could rely on to make the right decisions.

Next to him Louise sucked in her breath, a little half-conscious sound of consternation. He glanced at her, then to the screen where she was staring. The picture showed a small band of picketers who faithfully came every Saturday to an abortuary in De Kalb. The soundtrack described how a few faithful could fight death and selfishness just as much as a big group could: the key was commitment. The Pro-Life counselor was exhorting a girl in a lime green parka as she headed up the path to the death chamber entrance.

Each shot moved in closer to the head bent in fear and weakness. Simon knew this face without seeing, knew it by the color of the parka, by the way the fine brown hair parted over the bowed white neck. His bowels were softening and turning over and his throat was so dry he could only trust himself to whisper.

"You did this," he hissed to Louise under the flow of the soundtrack. She shook her head dumbly. "You knew about this. You knew about this and never told me." She only shook her head again, her eyes filled with tears. She turned to grab her napkin, turned so fast that she jarred the table and knocked a glass of water down the state representative's back.

The accident made her throat work with suppressed hysteria as she tried wiping her face, then the legislator's back. The state representative was gracious, helping to mop the front of her dress, laughing off the damp patch on his back, but Simon was sure he would be chuckling about him with other colleagues before the week was over: why should we listen to Simon? He can't even control his own wife.

Simon grabbed Louise's left arm and pulled her head down close to his mouth. "You go off to the ladies' room," he ordered in that same voiceless hiss.

"You leave now and don't come back until I'm through with my speech, you hear?"

Dumbly she pulled her arm away, apologizing through her tears to the state representative, dropping her handbag, spilling lipstick and Kleenex on the man's lap. The legislator patted her on the shoulder, tried to make out that he didn't mind, that it was an accident and he didn't need her to dry his back or pay to have his suit cleaned. She gave the man a fixed little smile and stumbled from the stage. If she'd practiced for a month she couldn't have done more to humiliate him.

The bishop leaned over and asked with unctuous concern if Louise was all right. Simon managed a twisted smile.

"She's fine. Just needs to go to the ladies'."

But he could kill her for this. Kill her for destroying him at his moment of triumph, for working hand in glove with the old man to get him. He really thought he'd die. That night he came home drunk from being out with his buddies and his daddy stood waiting by the refrigerator with a baseball bat.

You tell me one reason why I shouldn't use this on you, Simon Peter. The rock. The old man spat at him. The sand. I'm like a man who built his house on the sand. And Simon tried talking to him, tried making his voice come out big and booming to say he was a man, he could go out with his buddies if he wanted, but the only thing that came out was that terrible little squeak and then the old man was hitting him, hitting him so hard he ended up on the floor, peeing in his pants. He was lying on the floor all wet and bleeding and sobbing while his mother stood crying at the top of the stairs, her tiny voice pleading for him from the distance.

And all the while Sandra's silhouette mocked him from the screen. "One of our failures," the soundtrack intoned. "We didn't have the resources to give this girl the help she needed to choose Life. But with your support we'll be able to help other girls like this one, so that truly every life in this great land of ours will be held sacred."

My Mother's War

S. L. Wisenberg

My mother was an artist. When I was ten she entered her bone and glass period. I would eat pastrami sandwiches in the utility room, the thick smell of boiling beef fat in the kitchen permeating each bite. I held pickles to my nose like ether. Rings of white grease lined the double stainless steel sinks. She would stand, her French twist unraveling as she blew into the hollow end of a leg bone to free the marrow. The marrow was long and slimy inside the splintering bones, which were sharp as the shards of brown, clear and green glass she collected from the street. (You won't believe how much glass there is outside, she said. You better quit going around barefoot.) In the oven, they were supposed to melt together into the kind of threads that glassblowers produce. But it never got hot enough. She couldn't understand this. Why then, she asked, do people spend their money on Pyrex if any old glass in the oven doesn't break or melt?

She glued the glass to the bones. She filled their cavities with ground-up glass, the way other mothers filled turkeys with homemade dressing. She always bought chicken Kiev pre-stuffed. At other people's houses I would see mothers wrist-deep inside chickens as if they were caught, momentarily, in their own private patches of quicksand.

The reviewers came to the opening of her show. It was in a rented loft above a weaving factory. The man from the *Post* called it brilliant. The woman from the *Chronicle* said it was a sham. That her seven-year-old son working with her three-year-old spaniel could do better, except that they both had more sense than to play with broken glass.

A loudmouth TV anchor ridiculed her for three minutes on the five o'clock news and everyone I met after that said my name sounded familiar.

At her next show she strung baling wire through the bones. Black lights hung from fishnets. Everywhere was the smell of jasmine. The people who attended the opening were long-haired and bearded, wore muted flowing clothes and passed around hash pipes. The *Post* critic shared his Acapulco Gold.

Someone called the police.

The *Post* carried the story on the Arts page. The *Chronicle* put it on Page One. It was an open invitation, my mother said into the phone. We didn't station guard dogs at the door. Middle-class morality, she hissed after she slammed the receiver.

After that she always had to have two opening nights to accommodate the crowds.

Her hippies came to my Bat Mitzvah. My speech was about Jonah and the Whale. That was a violation. I knew it at the time. The story about Jonah is part of Yom Kippur. I was supposed to stick to the Torah portion. But that was about punishment for sorceresses and people who coveted. That's not something a child can relate to, my mother said.

I described the blubber inside the whale. Jonah almost drowned in the fat. This was more frightening than darkness. He felt like he was walking through slimy white mud, through melted chocolate, whipped cream cheese, cakes of softened soap. This was not manna. He could not eat any of it. He was looking for a righteous man. He struck a match and burned the top of the whale's insides. The whale blew him out his blowhole.

This proves, I told the congregation, that the search will save you.

Her hippies told her I was a deep thinker.

At the reception, I rested on a chair along the folding partition that separated the social hall from the sanctuary. A boy sat on my lap and fed me stale sponge cake. When he pinched my nipples and said, Milk Duds, I stood up.

He scampered away.

✦ ✦ ✦

By the time I was fifteen, she was famous. She flew to New York every two weeks. I lived on Sara Lee cheesecake and Mrs. Paul's fish sticks. In the afternoons I skipped algebra and sat on the sloping cement along the bayou and watched the overflow of the storm sewer. There was much green glass.

✦ ✦ ✦

Senior year I worked in a pet store. I changed straw every day and caught fish in my bare hands. The goldfish beat against my cupped palm like a heart pressed flat. I would take a deep gulp as I tossed it into a plastic bag. I exhaled as I tied the twist-em.

Don't overfeed her, I warned the earnest little kids.

She bought me a Nikon for graduation. She said, Do you want to take a year off? Not everybody goes to college.

I took one year and it grew to three, four, six. We count what we call life credits, the dough-faced lady at the community college said, like she was explaining the rules for hopscotch. You could get an A.A. degree in three months. What would you say your specialty is? Philosophy?

Two years later I became an artist-in-the-schools. My fingernails turned yellow and my hands always smelled acrid. I concentrated on portraiture. Look what you can do, I told the kids. Preserve what you see. Paint with light. Capture something and make copies forever.

I would fill in the pictures true-to-life with crayon and copy them on a color Xerox machine. They looked realistic, only somehow rougher. That became my trademark. Post-modern realism, they called it.

Her fame deserted her like a bored lover. She shaved her head and glued her hair to the wall in the living room. She separated the white strands from the black, burning the ends. This took an entire month. If you didn't look closely, it seemed like a small patch of zebra skin was attached to the wall over the couch.

She walked on glass-covered bones, barefoot, like an Indian brave.

I am trying to strengthen myself, she said.

I moved to the next state. I became active in community life. I worked my ten hours a month at the food co-op. I joined the artists' collective gallery. I took an "i" out of my last name. On Sundays I tutored migrant workers' kids. I taught them the game, rock-scissors-paper. Sometimes there was a waiting list for me in the artists-in-the-schools program. The students often sent thank-you notes.

When my mother died, her hippies came to the funeral in black suits. At home, they passed around joints and 'ludes. They brought homemade wine and Hershey bars. Chocolate, someone named Lydia said, has a chemical that uplifts you. That is the reason women eat it after breakups. It's therapeutic. Body wisdom.

You could have brought Toblerone, someone said, instead of some corporate product.

Aren't we supposed to boycott them? a man, someone's new lover, asked.

That's Nestlé, a skinny girl said.

The European bars are the best, said the man. I like Cherry Screams.

I think of chocolate-covered cherries. Inside the chocolate is a sugar crust, which holds in the sweet runny syrup and real fruit, round and still red. It is a house inside a house, a bunker, Jonah in his whale.

And what will you do? Cleo asked me, her smile a withered purple between tissue-thin wrinkles.

What I always do, I said.

She's been on her own for years, said someone I didn't recognize.

This is what she left: scrapbooks of clippings. Invitations to openings. Diploma from Pratt. The certificate of the *get*, the Jewish divorce.

And instructions for a new show. An environmental piece about the Holocaust. Posthumous. Something that would say, Conceived by Celeste Meyeroff, when it opened.

It needed a builder, someone to execute it, a general contractor sort of artist. I advertised in *Art News*, *American Artist*, *Present Tense* and small newsletters. It could be set up and shown anywhere. It was that kind of thing.

The best person lived two states north in a college town. I moved there; all places are the same. I became again an artist-in-the-schools. I located a color copying machine at the print shop downtown. I built another darkroom. On weekends I took pictures of traffic accidents and fires for the newspaper.

I helped the artist write the NEA for a grant application form. When she got the money I stopped returning her calls. I said I wanted to be surprised.

The artist invited me on the Sunday before the opening. She left the key to the gallery under the welcome mat. The door opened easily.

I was alone in a dark room. I stripped, like the sign said. The walls were cement block. A yellow lightbulb shown from the ceiling in a black cage. I felt it on my back like a sunlamp.

Metal claws snatched at my clothes. I was not given a claim check.

I waited for a voice over a loudspeaker. Instead I heard a xylophone, the melody from *All Things Considered*, cut short.

The light went out. I waited to sense bodies around me.

So what did you expect? I asked myself. This is the artist's conception of the Holocaust. Did you think she would manufacture crematoria? German kapos, shaved heads, lice—those are cliché. You expect these things. Your aunts and uncles, they didn't know what to expect. Didn't know about the showers. Or work camps.

They weren't really my aunts and uncles.

Someone's aunts and uncles. They could have been my relatives, if my great-grandfather had not left Poland. There had been a family dispute. Something about land. He was disowned.

So there will be no cattlecars. No stench. My mother made her Hell antiseptic.

What will the critics say?

Banal? Passé? The arts critic on the newspaper also covers drama, dance, photography, music (rock and classical), visiting authors and beauty pageant winners. I imagine her sitting at her desk, shuffling press releases with her long fingers that end in narrow slices of red. She smokes. Ashes sprinkle themselves on the white papers, filter into the crevices of the computer keyboard. One day the machine will refuse to mark on its screen and the repair man will be dispatched. He will find ash damage. The newspaper will be presented with an ethical problem: Was it her fault?

Yes. But the editor points out that the paper's medical insurance will cover the stop-smoking sessions at Mercy Hospital.

Walk five paces.
No wall.
Five more.
Run, hands out; whenever I float on my back at the Y, I always keep an arm extended to rasp against the concrete edge, saving my head. No wall. Counting to 1,000 I run to the left.
No wall.
Blessed art Thou, O Lord our God, King of the World, who has created the never-ending universe, extending far beyond our ken.
I begin in Hebrew: *Baruch ata Adonai*—but can remember only the blessings over Sabbath candles, wine and bread. And the generic, Thank You for enabling us to reach this season.

This is not our Sabbath. It is the Christian sabbath. The day that nothing is open but 7-Elevens. On Mondays, museums and beauty salons are closed. On Thursdays, retail outlets stay open till nine. Every night except Sunday, the downtown shopping mall is open till nine. White letters proclaim this on the glass doors in front of Penney's: These doors are to remain open at all times during business hours.
What happens to the employee who locks up early? A scolding. He is tired of traffic, of bag-laden shoplifters who graze from department to department, slipping in lacy Hanes and earrings that grow in sharp angles. The girls behind the counter promote these in

their many-pierced ears. Pink enamel triangles dancing on turquoise. Hoops. Gold balls.

The Nazis yanked out the Jewish teeth for gold.

The Jews at the foot of Sinai built a calf of gold.

What did Moses do with the calf?

What did the Nazis do with the gold?

Gold, we are told, is precious because it is fragile. Other elements must be added to bolster it. The human being holds trace elements of everything. Zinc. Uranium. Gold. Silver. Copper. Rubber. Paper, ink. Glass. Inside me is the universe. I am inside a microcosm.

My eyes are the color of a Seven-Up bottle, fragments shining in the sun. I loved my mother.

Her whispers coming from the loudspeaker: The exhibit is dedicated to my daughter, because she has been inside whales without a lantern. Behind her lids it is as dark as any Nazi midnight.

The Holocaust is a state of mind, the voice says.

It is wrong. I stand in her limitless night. No stars glitter like broken glass. Dear Lise, says the voice. This is what my world was like, except for the ten years when my arrangement of the discards of life and death brought me into the circus. I made something new and I was rewarded. But the audience went home.

She is attaching her loneliness to the six-million-fold horror of burning. My mother did not wear a tattoo, bore no more distinguishing a characteristic than the pain of abandonment. But even if the Holocaust was the human condition writ large, by attaching her wagon to that black star, she refused a chance at happiness.

I do not refuse mine. I do not rejoice at the mutilated: singed hair and broken bits of bone. I do not twist and fray what should be left to rest. I photograph what is. I keep the laws of kosher; I do not cook the lamb in its mother's milk. I do not attach like to unlike. I always focus before shooting.

Lise, you do not create, the voice says. You absorb. Now, I am blinding you with my sorrow.

The Holocaust, says the voice, is my story. It is your story. It is Jonah's story inside the whale.

I remember from my Bat Mitzvah speech: Seek, seek a way out. In the seeking is the answer.

The child's riddle comes back to me: What would you do if you were inside a brick house with scissors and a piece of paper?

Answer: Cut the paper in half. Two halves make a whole. Crawl out through the hole.

That is art.

To Those Who Come Behind Me

Sandra Jackson-Opoku

Ile-Ife, Nigeria

I've figured it out. If she were as long-lived as Big Momma was, then my great-grandmother's great-grandmother would be about 200 years old if alive today. Would have been between fifteen and twenty years old when she was captured across the ocean.

And I'm still searching. You do remember I was sent here? I came to the Mother of All Rivers with offering in hand and question in heart. My great-grandmother's great-grandmother was a saltwater woman. And somewhere within the lands and waters of West Africa, I know I will find her memory. I know it.

There is indeed a poetry in motion here, in the continually changing faces of land and women and men. The way grasses bend with the wind on the African savannah. The way men walk with men, and women

with women. Unashamedly holding hands in fast
friendship. The shine of the moon upon water at the
shrine of the River Goddess in this holy place.

Kwesi seems to know someone nearly everywhere.
He engineered our entry into the shrine long after it
had been closed to the public. It was past midnight
when his friend let us in. We were warned not to take
pictures or take anything away with us.

It's probably a personality disorder. I've been like
this since birth. No sooner would someone tell me not
to do something without giving me what I considered
adequate explanation, than I would feel immediately
compelled to go and do it.

Of course I sneaked and took the picture. It came
out beautifully, by the way. Even in the dark without
a flash, you could see the outline of a tranquil river in
the moonlight, the offering I brought a shadow upon
its bank. I'm still waiting to see how I'll be punished
for that particular sin. I think I've already received my
comeuppance for the other transgression.

I picked something up during our quiet walk in the
surrounding forest. A flattened, hairy pod I saw lying
on the forest floor. I picked it up and dropped it into
my purse as a souvenir. I still have it now, afraid to
touch it. Because soon after I first held the thing, the
palm of my hand burned and stung so, that it was
painful to take the pen and write these words.

Just call me Pandora. What spirits of evil did my
willfulness let loose? Perhaps my just punishment is
simply silence. A failure of the displeased goddess to
give immediate answer to the question I came to her
with.

"Kwesi, do you think it's the picture I took? Or the
thing I picked up? I must have offended her spirit.
Maybe I should go back and beg her forgiveness."

Kwesi shook his head in amused disbelief.

"Mae, you are certifiable. Come on, let's get back to Lagos. I've got the possibility of some work there. And you need a dose of reality. A nice, dirty, over-crowded city. A sane, rational university environment. You're taking this stuff too seriously."

Lagos, Nigeria

"Water, water everywhere," so said the ancient mariner.

And I can understand how a body could be over-whelmed by the sight of so much water, though I am by no means ancient, nor a mariner myself. I have seen the Atlantic, albeit from the air. I have traversed the Niger. Kunta Kinte's "Kamby Boloni." Visited the holy sanctuary of a sacred river said to be the temple of the goddess. And now it is lakes.

I am told *Lagos* is Portuguese for lakes. And this city is full of them, not lakes really but lagoons. Some of them are saltwater inlets of ocean. Others are fresh-water haunts of fishermen, like the ones Kwesi and I have discovered. The narrow beach is tucked away within the campus of the university and completely deserted, save the transparent jellyfish which wash ashore from time to time.

We have not had each other in two weeks. I had not realized how keenly I would miss the closeness of Kwesi's body next to mine. Not just the act, you know. There is something even more intimate than sex which comes from sleeping together. The ways in which two bodies meet in slumber, cupped or curled around each other. The way two heartbeats find the same rhythm. And I do swear that in sleeping head to head, you dream each other's dreams.

Kwesi has hunted up some kind of hustle here at Unilag. He is assisting in the editing of a new journal of African arts. A very exciting project. But our living arrangements are certainly not.

We have been staying in spartan student quarters at the university, strictly segregated by sex. It feels strange being back on campus after a decade, sharing rooms and showers with other women. Exchanging deodorant and nail polish and late night camaraderie. Not altogether unpleasant. But I do miss the closeness of nights with Kwesi.

So we have been prowling the campus, searching for a quiet spot where we can be alone. And stumbled upon this little strip of beach upon a lagoon. May I be blunt with you for a moment? When the surroundings are right, there is little need for foreplay.

Find this little spot for yourself, somewhere in a far corner of the compound of the campus of the University of Lagos. Come upon it just at the time of twilight when the sun and moon both share the same sky.

And let there be the sound of drums in the far-off distance. And arrange it so that just before loving, you catch sight of a night fisherman riding his craft. He flings out his nets; they hover briefly above the water like a low-flung constellation before settling into the element. And the wind will be a bit balmy, puffing the remnants of day into night. And see if you aren't both as ready as we were for each other.

Making offerings by rivers. Crossing over oceans. Loving by lagoons. So much water and so much confusion. Because Big Momma had been told in a dream to follow a certain river to a source of blood. And there she would find home.

How will I ever know which way of water is the one to follow?

Yaounde, Cameroon

Here in Cameroon I have seen my first African mountains.

I have been to the top of one and gazed upon a tranquil valley below, set between this range and the next. The lush greenness surrounding a volcanic lake in this nearly hidden space is so beautiful that the truth is hard to believe.

That the devastation of death and breathtaking beauty are sometimes blood brothers. That beneath that lake's tranquil surface the volcano's spirit still rumbles. And periodically emerges to spew the countryside with a poison stronger than napalm. A sulfuric gas that only five years before killed every man, woman, child and animal in the village. All save an infant whose very crying expelled poison from its lungs and saved its life.

The horror story haunts me for days. Maybe this is what has gotten me so jittery. I've become a walking accident waiting to happen. Incompetent with clumsiness.

We are here in the French-speaking capital, where Kwesi is doing work for, can you believe this? The International Girl Scouts organization. The man is a nomad and he takes his harvest wherever he finds it.

But I was telling you about this sudden, disconcerting attack of butterfingers. Elisa, the Anglophone Cameroonian woman with whom we are boarding, has taken to calling me "Dropping Things." It usually happens at mealtime. I have destroyed so many of her dishes and glasses it is shameful. At this rate we'll leave Yaounde next week deeply in debt.

The open-armed, full-hearted hospitality of Africa sometimes embarrasses me. I feel uncomfortable being waited upon hand and foot as a guest in another woman's home. Elisa is going to the office to work everyday, as is Kwesi. And I sit around idle, carefully instructed to lift my finger in no household task. I feel like Minnie the Moocher. And I tell Elisa so.

"Fine," she answers, retiring to her room to read. "You will prepare the evening meal."

Now, I have never been the best of cooks. I think it's an act of rebellion from childhood. I cooked for the whole family from the age of eight on. The task was always an intrusion when I wanted to be off in a library reading, or at the kitchen table writing something down. In fact, almost anything was preferable to tending hot pots. And as soon as I went away to college and didn't have to do it anymore, I deliberately lost the knack of cooking.

And now a slave of American labor-saving devices, I have burned my meals with the best of them. Aided by gas stoves, food processors, and microwave ovens. What can I possibly do in Elisa's kitchen with a strange one-burner stove hooked up to a bottle of propane?

I decide to keep it simple. Fried plantains and eggs. I peel the plantain, careful to scrape away all the tough inner fiber I have heard can be toxic. I slice it into uniform circles. And wonder of wonders! I am able to operate the stove without asking for instructions. I heat up a pan of palm oil and fry the plantain perfectly. Perfectly! Crisp and light brown around the edges, without burning.

I crack open six or seven guinea fowl eggs, just the right number for three people. They are tiny, brown-flecked things I can never get used to after the almost obscene ovalescence of the American supermarket variety. I whip them up frothy and add to them hot peppers which sting my fingers as I mince them. The chopped bits of tomato stain the mixture with curious bloody streaks.

I reheat the oil in which the plantain was fried. The eggs are scrambled adequately, thick and yellow, still with those bloody streaks. But looking delicious and smelling better. I turn off the burner and turn to slice a loaf of the French bread on the table. French bread, mind you, baked by a real Frenchman. There are plenty of Europeans living in Yaounde, much more so than in any of the other places we've visited.

As I stretch for the bread I hear an ominous crashing behind me. And I turn to see my carefully prepared pan of eggs, steaming upended on the floor. Elisa has appeared in the door, book in hand. Almost gloating. "I knew I could never trust an American woman alone in my kitchen," her smug smile seems to say.

"What now, 'Dropping Things?'"

And I can only shrug my helplessness.

"I don't know what happened. It just fell. At least nothing's broken."

Elisa helps me to salvage the top layer of eggs, untouched by the floor. We stoop over the spill with spoons and plates.

"You know," Elisa tells me, "if I were from the villages and superstitious, I'd tell you why you are always dropping food."

"Why?" I throw my hands open to the air. "Tell me, so I can figure how to stop doing it."

"That your ancestors were hungry and wanted to be fed. That's what I'd believe if I were a superstitious woman from the villages."

Elisa was a new breed of African woman. College-educated, city-dwelling, living on her own in a city without family. I didn't know if she was superstitious or not. But I had enough of it for both of us. And as I threw the discarded eggs to the cannibal chickens who clucked at the back, I thought of one particular ancestor squatting by strangers' doors, gaunt with famine.

Here in the vastness of West Africa, of mountains and deserts and rivers and savannah, how would I ever find my way to her? So that her hungry spirit might be fed?

In air, en route from Yaounde, Cameroon to Accra, Ghana

Kwesi is very impatient with what he considers my acquired superstitions. The willingness of an otherwise intelligent woman to suspend disbelief and embrace the possibilities of an other reality.

He also questions the importance of this mission of mine to find my African roots.

"You know that you are of Africa. Why this desperate determination to connect to a particular place, when all of Africa can be yours? What difference does it make what village one of your ancestors hailed from?"

"But these beads, Kwesi. They are my connection to something particular. They were brought to America by my great-grandmother's great-grandmother. Probably worn on the slave ship that brought her over. I know that she came from somewhere here in West Africa. And I need to know her story. She is the one I've got to find."

"But what about your other ancestors? Those of Africa, and those of other places? Don't you want to know their stories, too?"

"I can't go chasing every star in the sky. I've got to follow this one."

Kwesi is a paradox. He wants to reason me out of my wanderings, yet he is always willing to lead me on them. I can't seem to make him understand that it is not just the unspoken promise I made to Big Momma on her death bed. That what guides my wanderings is a faith which cannot be measured by reason. And I will find the river where blood is born, or I will die trying.

Accra, Ghana

Love is like the earth, layered with so many levels of meaning. And hate can be as clean and deadly as a laser. But jealousy is such a sloppy emotion. A muddy pond mixed with the stirred-up sediments of love and hate and fear.

I ran into a paragraph from my past. Not a chapter, not even a page. Just a sentence or two in the overall story. Kwesi knew that a particular man had been my dearest misery for almost half my life. And he knew that I was still getting over it. But I never told him just who that man was. So when we met the African author, he just assumed.

This is not the first time the African author was the object of another man's jealousy. The other man was Trevor. And this story rightly belongs in the Trevor chapters of the book.

Trevor had a sweet tooth. Other men eyeing what he considered his private store of goodies brought that out in him. Once, at an autograph party for a West African author visiting campus, I enjoyed a long, mildly flirtatious conversation with the guest of honor. I had been properly awed and he had been sufficiently flattered.

He talked about African literature. I questioned him avidly. He told me it was time for all African-Americans to come home. From that come-hither sparkle in his eye, he must have thought this particular African-American could benefit from a get-acquainted course.

And Trevor, watching from the other side of the room, shot suspicious glances in our direction. Finally he stood and beckoned me away.

"Mae. Come over here."

And I got up to leave, quick to answer the call of my master's voice. But the African author had caught my hand.

"Will you come to the festivities tonight?"

Trevor had bounded across the room to separate his hand from mine.

"Comrade," he scolded. "This is my woman."

And he had taken me straight home. Undressed me summarily and laid me across his perfectly made bed. For a man Trevor was very neat. Made perfect hospital corners.

Standing fully clothed above the bed, he addressed me. Sternly professorial.

"This is mine, woman." His hand wound into the briar patch between my legs. "My little honey pot. I'm the first one to taste it and I want to be the last. Don't want no other man stirring around in there."

"Yes sir." I had deferred demurely. This was fifteen years ago, remember. My submissive stage. "But if you want to you can stir it up a little yourself."

> Will you quench me when I'm hungry?
> Cool me down when I'm thirsty?
> Your recipe darling, is so tasty.
> And you sure can stir your pot.
> Stir it up, little darling . . .

I couldn't hear that Bob Marley tune again without thinking about Trevor and the honey pot. And experience a little bit of shame to have been flattered by his jealousy and to have mistaken it for a sign of love. To have been so possessed with, and willing to be possessed by one man. But bear in mind that I was young and impressionable and he was my first lover. Bear in mind that he was a greedy grizzly, devouring the nectar of one pot until he tired of the taste. And moving on to sample the sweetness of other flowers. Jasmine, Sassafras, Sunflower.

I didn't mean to digress so into the sweetbitter memory of that man. Because this is now Kwesi's story and mine. Trevor has been left behind and it is Kwesi's scent I'm wearing now. But jealousy still looms, even here.

We ran into the African author again. This time at some evening for faculty at the University in Legon. He did not remember me and I would not have remembered him had he not a public name outside of himself. And still he was smooth as oil, as flirtatious as ever.

I entertained the party with my tales of Big Momma and Nana, her African ancestor. Avoiding the skeptical roll of Kwesi's eyes, I told them I was in Africa trying to discover her origins.

And the African author became very interested. Insisted that I show him the 200-year-old beads which were an integral part of this history. I lifted my top a bit to reveal them coiled like a blue snake around my waist. The African author reached out and touched them. He told me that beads identical to these were used in his village to this very day. Not, so far as he knew, to mark adolescent girls' onset of puberty, but to hold up the diapers of babies.

"Of course you haven't connected with your ancestors. You have been looking in the wrong place. Nigeria, Cameroon, Senegal. Everyone knows that *Nana* is an Akan word. It means old man, old lady. Grandmother. You are home now."

I was beside myself with excitement. A lead! A clue! I fell upon the African author, questioning him about beads and rivers and anything I could think of that could give me something more to go on.

He smiled disarmingly, taking my face and tilting it in his hands.

"Do you know, you look so much like an Ashanti woman. Your skin is very dark, and we Ashantis believe that the blacker a person's skin, the closer the person is to the earth, to the ancestors, to the gods. You could almost be my cousin."

Kwesi snorted in his jollof rice. It was quite common for both of us to be assured that we were descended from this or that particular nation. People know I am not from their place, but something in me makes them think I am from somewhere nearby. I'd been told on innumerable occasions by dozens of people that I was certainly Wolof or Hausa or Fulani or Mandinka or another member of a neighboring nation.

But even Kwesi would have to admit it. When I took a good look at the African author, I realized that we did look something alike. Slim builds, dark skins, long necks, round faces.

He said that he must know how to contact me. All in pursuit of cultural inquiry, of course. I must go to Kumasi and consult with the elders at the palace of the Asantehene. He was certain someone there could help. And he could help on this end with a contact, a letter of introduction. When the evening was over, I realized I'd spent it all in the company of the African author. Kwesi was uncharacteristically quiet on the ride to our lodgings.

And that night in bed he turned away from me.

"Maybe you should have fallen in love with a native-born African man."

"Why?" I questioned, climbing to his side of the bed to see his face. "Why would you say that?"

"He would have so much more to give you than I."

"Like what?" I wanted to know.

"Whatever it is you need so badly. A sense of belonging, of finding yourself."

If Trevor acted out his jealousy in possessiveness, Kwesi's was played out in misery and martyrdom. I was having none of it.

"I'm not looking for myself in somebody else. I don't need you or any other man to tell me who I am. I know who I am."

"Do you, Mae?" This was a new side of Kwesi. Depressed, morose. "Then why are you here in Africa? Looking for yourself outside of yourself."

"But Africa isn't outside of me," I insisted. "It is in me. And I am in it. It is my genealogy."

We argued on into the night. Kwesi telling me I was romanticizing the motherland, glorifying the past I did not understand and could never fully know. Asked me if I realized that this very type of *agri* bead I wore around my waist had been used as currency in the precolonial era. Had helped turn one African people against another, used for trade in whiskey and guns and slaves. Told me to contemplate the possibility that one woman's freedom might have been used to finance the decoration of another woman's body.

He even threw this one in my face. I had confessed to him that I'd always been attracted to other-born African men before meeting him. Men whom I perceived to have a sense of wholeness I did not. Men who owned themselves; that way at least one of us would. He said I was placing the same impossible burden on the back of Mother Africa.

Oh, he was very discouraging. Told me I was looking for a needle in a haystack, a grain of sand in the desert. Said that even a tumbleweed had roots. Asked when I was going to stop chasing the wind. I tossed his question back at him.

"When are you?"

He smiled. And I realized that he had not been arguing with me all night, but himself. Because it was he who chased the wind. I was the one who followed rivers. Which can be unpredictable, too. Full of surprises and unexpected twists.

"That's different, Mae. I'm a professional wanderer. I've been at it so long I've forgotten what I set out looking for."

"So why are you trying to discourage me? Maybe I'm a nomad too. Maybe we were meant to wander together."

Kwesi shook his head ruefully, examining my face as if it were his own.

"I don't know. Maybe I care too much about you to feed your fantasies. Or maybe I envy you the energy which gives purpose to your wanderings. Which makes them less aimless than mine. Maybe I don't want you to find what you're looking for because then you won't need me anymore."

Can you believe this man?

"Kwesi." The time was past for talking. It would be morning soon and no loving had gone on. "I've been looking for you all my life. What do you mean I won't need you? I'll need you then. And I need you now. Right now."

I think Trevor is out of my system now. I'm going to say this last one thing about him and hope I won't have to mention his name again.

Because he was the first man I had loved, and because I loved him for such a very long time, he had become the standard against which all subsequent lovers were judged. His height, his size, his eyes, his intellect. His style in bed. I unconsciously measured all my men against Trevor and usually found them wanting. Until Kwesi. Because Kwesi was so entirely opposite, and so much his own man.

Do you remember the song Aretha used to sing? Oh, I listened, clasping the lyrics to my heart when I was young and stupid.

Though you don't call anymore,
I sit and wait in vain.
I guess I'll rap on your door,
tap on your window pane.
I'm gonna prove to you, baby
the changes I've been going through
missing you. Listen you.

Until you come back to me,
that's what I'm gonna do.

Music was the meter that gave rhythm to our lives.
That fueled our struggle from the day we stepped
shackled feet on bloody shores. But most of our love
songs are all wrong, you know. Telling us to do the
wrong things, to feel the wrong ways. To be cool
when we should be hot. Foolish when we should be
wise. And when we take that message and internalize
it, it can mess us up for life. Thinking that loving is
supposed to hurt. That men are to be worshipped and
women mastered.

Loving doesn't hurt with Kwesi. It is easy to know
him, easy to love him. He is not like Trevor. He is not
tall. In fact he's exactly my height, maybe even an
inch shorter. Who wears dreadlocks and glasses. Not
the sexy wire frames or aviator style, but old-fashioned horn-rimmed spectacles.

He is a man who asks more questions than he gives
answers. Who has not Trevor's studied style in bed,
but who comes to me eager, sometimes clumsy with
tenderness. And whose vulnerability lies just beneath
the surface of his skin.

I sense in him a person who has been hurt, maybe
hurt badly. But still is not afraid to love. And that is
what I love so much about him.

Legon, Ghana

Well, the River Mother has answered me. Not the answer to the question I've been seeking, but an answer all the same. When I was first sent to the Mother of all Waters I didn't realize this same spirit was a goddess of fertility.

You know they say that one member of every family will turn out to be barren? I always figured I was one of them. I've been sexually active for something like sixteen years now. For the past ten of them I haven't used anything. And never got pregnant. Not until now.

It is entirely unexpected and a bit of a problem. Telling Kwesi won't be. That's the thing about him, the wonderful thing. He is so accepting a man. He takes you as you are. Bony ribs. Bad breath and evil attitude in the morning. Beliefs he calls superstitions. Whatever is part of you he accepts as part of the package.

No, telling Kwesi won't be the problem. The problem will be knowing whom to tell. I did say I wouldn't mention Trevor's name again, but this changes things, doesn't it?

But then, that is not for you to worry about. You have much bigger and harder questions in your time I am sure. You have an earth to save and worldwide wounds to heal. The fractured legacy we have left you to mend. Let me not add to that burden more than you can bear.

Surely you will want to know why I am here. In the heart of Africa. Wearing a worn cotton blouse and lappa that feel good against my skin. Sitting beneath the generous shade of a mango tree. Holding this pen and page, pausing only to swat flies or simply think about what it is I want to say to you.

Do you know that in this home of Kwesi's friends, who are musicians and batik artists, one of the wives knew of you before I knew myself? She smiled at me and patted my flat belly.

"You de get picken."

I asked her what made her think I was pregnant. I showed no signs of it, save missed periods in a cycle that was never regular in the first place. I was in fact thinner that I had ever been. And I wanted to know how she knew.

"Some of us," she said smiling, "we can smell it."

What is the scent of fecundity? Is it something you can smell yourself, curled there within the waiting place? Is it rich like ripening fruit? Or loamy, like the delta soil which rises out of rivers?

I feel myself balanced at the apex of a pyramid whose base is buried in centuries of sand. And a wind has just come to blow the years away. Or perhaps I am in the midleaf of a thick book. The years unfolding both behind and before me. And I in the middle of a story I know neither the beginning nor the ending to.

Did she, the one I seek, ever wonder as I do? About her future. Who and what her generations would be. Would her descendants live to shame or glorify her name? And who exactly was this first mother? How far do you go back before all humankind is linked? And how did Eve, if you believe in her, learn to mother when she was not mothered?

What would it have been had the seed never left these shores? What would I have been had my branches grown and spread out only on this side of the Atlantic? Would I have been the same person? Had the same need to tell stories to try to make sense of the puzzling world? Would I have had the where-withal to do it?

But it is useless speculating this way. Because I am who I am and you will be who you are. You, the ones who come behind me. The one within me waiting and the ones waiting within her. Or him. My generations spread out beyond me. The base of the pyramid which holds me up.

The time will come when you will hunger as I have hungered, for a sign that reassures you that there is some link between you and your past. And I will be your past. So what I wish to say to you is this.

Listen to the click of your story beads. Know that there is drumbeat in your blood, and know too the source of this drumbeat. Know that blood comes before birth and also after death. Blood is the living lifeline, the river that connects us. Your heartbeat is river music, dear ones of my blood. Keep your ear tuned to the pulse of it.

The Country of Herself

Sharon Solwitz

The sidewalk is wide enough for four to walk abreast, but the man passes so close his arm brushes her arm. Too light for a jostle, too quick for sleaze, but she feels stung. It has happened to her before, this piece of foreign rudeness, in this same dress so long and loose it's almost a *chador,* but not with baby Ike in his pack around her neck. She lifts the front pack and airs her chest, then kisses the brim of his little blue hat. Perhaps it has to do with what she read in the paper this morning, Israel's capture of an important Muslim cleric. Or her red hair flaming out from all these covered heads. Her arms in her short sleeves? The sensation lingers on the back of her arm like a bug bite. She says to her husband, "Win, I am hating this place."

"What place do you like?"

"Oh stop."

The man's *khafiyeh,* loose white shirt and incongruous European-style vest blur into a group of

199

similar outfits. The air over the street is hot and damp, too thick to breathe let alone talk through. She argues inside herself. Jerusalem she loved for the smell of the stone, and London for the constant motion of the streets, and Madison, Wisconsin, where she met Win and married him, for the light wind that made her skin hum with the pleasure of feeling. In Baghdad the wind blows a gray yellow dust tinting the windows and sidewalks and the men's white pajama suits and even the skin of her arms. In Baghdad your skin isn't yours, she feels, but the property of the insects and men about town who desire it. Wear long sleeves. Do not scratch no matter how bad the itch. Breathe shallowly.

That's how she talks, simple words, hardly any accent. But he has to think about what she says and even then he isn't sure he has it figured out. She walks a half step ahead of him, always faster than he walks: Dvora Wallace née Blank. Fill in the Blank, he sometimes says to her, a joke. In pain there's an element of Blank, she once said. From Emily Dickinson. A little grim, but her style, *her* joke, he thinks. Baghdad is no worse, ladies and gentlemen of the jury, than some of the other places they've lived. Despair is her dramatic art, statements like all she wants of a place is the right to go crazy without anyone staring. Not that it's exactly easy here for her, being Israeli, but they aren't planning to spend their lives, probably not more than another year. She simply likes to startle. It gives her power at dinner parties, though it bothers some people, himself included. "Why do you talk like that?" he said to her once, explaining that it came across to him and many people as intentionally cryptic. And she said with anger at the bottom of her voice that she didn't know "many people" and it was not at all "cryptic" (sneering at his word) for people whose minds weren't spoiled by all day sucking up to assholes. Not fair, he still thinks. Or at least there are kinder ways to put it. He knows how to use warmth and persistence and the velvety edge of power dealing with folks not born to Western ways of business—getting utilities hooked up, for example, by native service people for whom contracts are as binding as New Year's resolutions, and at the end they still like him, the company heads and the native contractors; nothing to be ashamed of. He's happy till he has a good reason not to be and he doesn't mess with other people's good moods. "I try to be tactful," he said to Dvora. To which she replied, "Your mind is spoiled by tact." Now what was that supposed to mean?

The itch is under the pack, between her breasts, where she cannot scratch. She wonders whether it's an old itch or a new one in the making. Either way there's nothing she can do. Baby Ike wakes up and starts to cry.

"He's hungry," Win says.

"He cannot be hungry," she says. She'd nursed him in the apartment half an hour ago. She puts his pacifier back in his mouth.

"He's so white," Win says. "Do you think he's sick?"

"He is not sick." She lifts the brim of his baby hat. On his temple, showing pale blue through the skim-milk colored skin is a pattern of veins radiating out from a circle like a child's drawing of the sun. "It's your shadow," she says. "His skin looks blue in your shadow over him."

Win bends down and kisses Ike's cheek with so much force the baby squawks. She inserts the pacifier a second time. "Your kiss is a punch sometimes," she says. "A left to the jaw!" She pats Win's cheek, demonstrating how to touch softly, though as far as she can see, he doesn't feel light touches. To arouse him she must do to him what would cause her pain. Sometimes she thinks he has no nerve endings in his skin. "I will dye my hair brown," she says.

"Please don't."

"I want something to eat," she says.

"It's Ramadan, there's no place open."

"Even when it is not Ramadan."

One of the things she hates about Baghdad is the near total absence of restaurants. Though she isn't really hungry. She just wants something like padding over her nerve endings, which feel too exposed. Alongside this main street and affixed to many of the buildings are larger-than-life paintings of a mustached man in various costumes, the country's president, staring at her. The street is crowded with men who stare at her, and though they do not speak or gesture she feels their feeling for her, their what-would-be loathing if she were significant enough to loathe. If she weren't an infidel and a woman. A Jewish woman in a country where Jews (the 300 remaining) aren't allowed to own their homes. A Jewish woman from a country that, unprovoked, bombed a nuclear plant in this country, reported to be making bombs and not electricity, and although she wasn't convinced—had in fact written a letter deploring the attack, which the *Post* had printed—it wouldn't have helped her get a visa. Jewish tourists can't get visas here—Jews and people with AIDS, she has discovered; five days after they arrived they'd had to take an AIDS test, which did not, thank God, expose her nationality. On her application she'd lied about her nationality, also her religion, her father's name, her grandfather's name; carrying her visa now she sometimes wonders who she is. No one knows she's Jewish-Israeli but it's hard enough being a Western woman, perhaps significant enough or something enough to be taken hostage and traded for the newly-captured Muslim cleric. "I need a chador," she says.

"You'd look silly in a chador."

Actually, she doesn't want a chador, which stands for a good part of what appalls her. Actually, she wants to tear off her clothes and scratch where she isn't allowed to scratch, her crotch, and under her milk-heavy breasts. "A chador would hide my hair," she says.

"Let's go back to the apartment."

"The apartment is death."

"Do you want me to carry the baby? I'll be glad to."

"He's fine where he is."

"You have great hair," he says. "It would be a sin to hide your hair."

He works to humor her but out of selfishness, she thinks, to protect his own good mood. She holds his arm even though she's angry with him. She is so often angry with him she can't afford to act on it anymore. So she holds him fiercely. Calls him sweet names. Feels her anger in her eyes, making ugly things uglier, the greasy dust on the bolts of fabric in the store window she is passing. And maybe also, her anger, on her wrists and ankles, which itch so intensely now it feels like burning. The sun eats through the opaque white sky, burning her arms, her head through her hair, the tops of her feet around the leather thongs of her sandals. Clumsy around the front pack, she's rummaging through her bag for her sunblock when a man pushes by on the storefront side of the walk, the fabric of his sleeve glancing across her arm. "Shit, Win! They are doing it on purpose!"

"Let's go over to the Sheraton," Win says. "We can sit in the coffee shop."

"I want to go back to America. Why cannot they send you where is respect for women?" She is speaking loudly. Two men walking in front of them stop, turn. "Mind your fucking business!" she says.

"It's a good thing they don't speak English," Win says.

"Why do you not talk to them? Apologize to them for my hot head?"

The men continue to stare at her, stock still on the sidewalk, holding onto each other's hands, with an impassivity that transcends, or so it seems, the language barrier. She makes a face at them. They do not respond.

"I think they are autistic," she says loudly.

Win pulls her away then, whispering, "Do you want to start a fight?"

"I want *you* to start a fight, Mister America."

He squeezes her hand. "Try and calm down, Dvora. Let's go back to the apartment and play gin rummy."

She looks him dead in the eye. "My skin itches. Do you understand? I want to take it off and throw it in the fire and burn it."

He says something she doesn't hear. The dusty wind is blowing, the *shamal*, the dry northwest wind that never stops. She runs back to the store with the bolts of cloth in the window and buys enough for a chador.

He waits in the sun patiently like an ox. He thinks of himself as an ox; he can take physical pain, extremes of hot and cold. Once he'd wanted to be an astronaut. But Dvora weighs on him. He feels her unhappiness as strain in one of his shoulders.

Not that he blames her. The people on the street act like assholes at times. But she struts her unhappiness so that it spills over onto him, not to mention the people who have invited them into their homes: good people, at worst a little close-mouthed, who've gone out of their way to make him and Dvora feel comfortable. His only problem with them is that they don't appreciate his style of joke. Once he made a kidding remark about their street art, all those faces of Big Brother Hussein (counting, one afternoon, he'd reached 250, honest to God) making it hard for him to run a stoplight. Not haha funny maybe, but no one had even smiled.

He takes off his sportcoat, shakes off the dust, then puts it back on, a little annoyed with Dvora now. He didn't force her to come here. They could have gone to Lahore or Copenhagen; Baghdad was her choice despite the official anti-Semitism. She called it "the land of my fathers." She wanted to find the Iraq beneath Iraq, the Iraq of the Bible, where Abraham was born, married, heard the word of the Jewish God and demolished the idols. There was something for her to discover here. She had said that fiercely, forehead shining. He'd imagined that if he touched her at that moment her skin would burn him.

She stands in the doorway of the fabric shop while Win helps her drape the black swatch over her head and shoulders. The shape is wrong, she thinks—too rectangular. And it needs a hem. And she has to hold the sides together and out from below her chin so Ike can breathe. But despite the heat and the baby's weight on her neck, in the shelter of the makeshift chador she seems to float along the street, as if what-

ever happens from now on is happening to someone
not her. "Bella, bella," Win says. "*Azeh yofee!*"

She takes one edge of the fabric between her teeth
like the veiled women in Damascus, a frame for their
dark eyes, long straight noses, thin upper lips.

"I must have you," Win whispers.

She laughs. The fabric slips from her mouth and
falls to the ground behind her. Win restores it.

"Let's go back to the apartment," he says.

"In a little," she says. "I need the exercise."

"I'll give you some exercise."

Part of her wants to comply, to feed this small burst
of his feeling for her. But she likes her own feeling of
being in costume, even in the narrowing streets, the
thickening crowds of the old covered market they are
nearing. "Ike is enjoying our walk," she says.

"Ike is sleeping," Win says.

"He will wake up when we remove him from the
pack."

She kisses Win's neck as a small apology, then
bends down and kisses Ike on the configuration of
veins on his temple, so delicate that sometimes even
lips seem too forceful, and only when she looks up
does she notice the crowd that has gathered around
them. It's made up entirely of men, perhaps five deep
already, clotting into a circle.

"Keep moving," Win says. "Toward the apartment."

He puts his arm around her shoulders, John Wayne
Wallace, she can tell he's scared. She is not scared;
she's looking for the words to shoo these people away.
The words refuse to assemble, though; maybe she is
nervous, a little. There isn't much room in the eye of
their personal hurricane, eight or ten feet, the radius
of the circle free of mustached men in khafiyehs and
loose white pants, in vests scavenged, maybe, from the
business suits of Western hostages. The scavengers
don't speak, not even to murmur to each other. They

simply move along as *they* move along, staring, not at Win but at her—hair, face, bare arms—worse than disapprovingly, the way a child stares at a cripple or a dwarf. She feels a pulse of almost-fear but doesn't try to cast it off—it seems to relieve her skin's itching, her rage at these men, who will stone a woman to death for adultery, guiltlessly, self-righteously, enacting the will of a God who guiltlessly, self-righteously ordains the woman's death for that crime but not the man's. She stares back brazenly now—she is not a Muslim woman—and slips out from under Win's arm. And as she removes herself, as she takes a step unattached, with her infant son but free of her husband, a man in white who looks like all the other men in white breaks the circle and pulls off her chador.

She screams. Baby Ike starts crying. She screams in Hebrew, her first language, "Give me it, you fucking fruit-bastard!" yelling as she shoves him from behind. It's a controlled shove, not enough to make him fall, just enough to register her anger, but his body, soft, falls back with surprising ease into the crowd. She watches, amazed for a moment at the power of her hands. She wants to see his face. She wants to see what she has made him feel. What of her has registered on him. Embarrassment, perhaps? Humiliation? No emotion that she can fathom. With a blank face, hardly looking at her, he takes a step toward her and spits. At her. On her. On the pleated front of this white linen dress she will never wear again. She's screaming words she has never used, Arab curses she always knew but would have been punished for using at home.

"Dvora, stop!" Win cries.

She pauses a second, waiting for him to do something—she isn't sure what—one of the violent things he must have learned from American television. But

his face looks wounded and spit at as she is sure hers
is not. She picks up the chador and cleans her dress
with it like a rag, then casting it away, she pushes
through the crowd, which closes behind her like the
door of a house she has left forever. She's not scared
at all running with Ike against her chest, running fast,
zigzagging down alleys like an Arab boy who has
thrown stones, though she was the one stoned, no?
and running for her life with Ike thumping in his front
pack, till the streets widen and empty and she has him
alone.

But Dvora liked to run off. From movies, the
houses of friends, from fancy restaurants. It was not
unusual. If he said something wrong, that didn't come
up to the intensity of her own feeling, she'd get up
from the table and leave him alone with his food. The
first time he didn't even pay the check, he jumped up
and ran after her. The second time he put a bill on the
table, catching up to her near their apartment in
Madison; it took a while to calm her down. The third
time he finished his dinner, coming home to find her
so enraged she threw a shoe at him and drove off in
their car. He would have called the police if he hadn't
known she wanted him to call the police, had choreo-
graphed that dance in order to make him.

Later, weeping, she described to him how she'd
driven round and round and round the block. But,
ladies and gentlemen of the jury, he says, is he responsible for that? There was something awry in the way
she processed information. According to a theory he
heard, the presence of the enemy—all those Arabs
pressing in on that long hallway of a country—was
supposed to diminish the personal ego, unite citizens
in service of a common cause. But Dvora was as self-

absorbed as any American he knows. Clearly she was
spoiled; her family extra-privileged, dad official consul
to the American Midwest—doors open for her; mucho
cultural glitz. And then her personal early glory—an
IQ called off the charts, with subsequent inordinate
respect from adults. But every year or two her mother
would go "vague" (Dvora's word) and vanish for a
while to some fancy sanitarium—maybe she didn't get
enough love, or enough consistent, the right kind?

He walks away from the window, the dusty gray-
green of the trees in the little park across street, hearing Dvora's response. "Amateur psychology." She
threw that at him once. "Puerile analysis." Probably it
is. It doesn't make him any happier with his wife,
who, for whatever reason, seems to perceive her half
of anything as the smaller portion. Dvora, the Israeli,
from the place God picked out for the people He
picked out of all the peoples of the earth, all the
idolaters, the *gentiles*. How was an ordinary gentile
supposed to respond to that? What about his feelings,
his stomach in knots at restaurants and movies, not
knowing what chance remark, what failure on his part
to laugh or cry at the right time would bring on the
big guns? He feels bad for not having managed to find
her on the streets of Baghdad, worse than bad, but
she's a grown woman with a will and a temper that
can lay him flat—he shouldn't have to take all the
blame.

She is almost euphoric on the anonymous street, a
feeling she hasn't had in so long it makes her throat
tight. Directly across from her and behind a little
stone bench is a portrait of the Iraqi president with
a smile on his face, kissing the hand of someone's
baby. Seated on the bench two head-scarved young

men with hard, handsome jaws vie for the honor of directing her to the train station, their Arabic as clear and pure as Hebrew to her ears.

Her elation continues on the train, though there are no empty seats, and the windows are so grimy she can barely see out. Ike, asleep around her neck, seems to weigh nothing at all. There are women on the train—perhaps a third of the passengers, and the first she has seen with animated faces. Within the shelter of their chadors they are talking to each other, unlike the women who hurry along the city streets looking straight out in front of them like horses. These women might answer her if she asked them a question. They might forgive her bare arms and tell her the address of a good jewelry shop, the name of a responsible person to help with the baby. That they don't look at her now doesn't feel hostile for some reason; she is an outsider here but not an enemy. None of the men offer her their seat but that doesn't seem hostile either, not even rude, simply innocent. Their innocence is a filmy scarf around her, rendering her and her baby pleasantly invisible. She could ride this train almost indefinitely, at least for the 300 miles to Kuwait.

What she will do in Kuwait isn't clear yet. She has heard how Western it is, the past and poverty, the righteous fierceness of the religion, all covered over with oil money. Perhaps she will eat Kentucky Fried Chicken there. She will buy a huge box of disposable diapers. She will stay at the Kuwaiti Sheraton, take a hot shower, sit on a disinfected toilet seat, sleep between soft sheets on a mattress that never knew a flea, and decide whether to return to Baghdad or Jerusalem or the United States.

They are at the outskirts of Baghdad now. A few passengers debark, but more get on the train, pushing her to the back. She is not particularly tired, just beginning to be hungry, when Ike starts to cry. She looks at

her watch. It is a while since he has eaten. And he
needs to be changed. Her heart starts to beat with
almost-panic. She can nurse him—in fact her breasts
are starting to ache—but she doesn't know the proto-
col, especially during Ramadan. One of the other
women is holding a baby but older than hers; earlier
she'd watched him chew on an orange. Perhaps eating
during the day is permitted young Muslim children,
just as Jewish children are exempted from fasting on
Yom Kippur. She could nurse modestly if she were
seated: Concealed by pleats in her dress front are the
appropriate slits. But standing in the aisle of this
crowded train she might inadvertently expose herself,
an accident for which the Koran, no doubt, decreed a
large penalty. She thinks of the two meters of fabric
she bought, trampled on the street now, or perhaps
already scavenged, already cut and almost sewn into a
long black skirt, an apron, a shroud? Ike's crying gets
louder. Some people are looking at her, nibbling at her
anonymity. She squeezes along the aisle in the hope of
transferring cars, though she isn't sure she can transfer
while the train is moving, or even if the doors open.
Then at the far back of the car a man stands up from
his seat. He's wearing a complete Western business
suit, a gray matching jacket and pants. He is not wearing a khafiyeh. "Hello!" he calls out, pushing the man
beside him over a little.

"I speak English!" she cries. "Do you speak
English?"

"Such very good English," he says. "Please, Missus
with the beautiful baby, please to sit down on this
very fine seat. You are to Babylon going? To see the
fabulous Hanging Gardens, yes?"

He used to like this, the something Wild West about her, but in their little apartment chock-full of objects she's taken a shine to, books she has started and not finished, it's making him mad, how she always chooses the path of greatest resistance.

There is a pattern. In Israel where women serve in the army she was a conscientious objector. Her first boyfriend was a Palestinian kid she called "my sweet lizard" and slept with (she'd said) on and off for a couple of years. She married a WASP, for God's sake, himself Winston Charles Wallace of Rosedale, St. Paul, Minnesota. She called herself a failed Israeli. But she has one thing in common with every Israeli he's ever met—she wears her personality on her hip like a sixgun.

Not even Jehovah was safe from her. There was a Bible story where God asked Abraham for the life of his only son. God backed off in the end and let Abraham sacrifice a ram, and probably He never wanted the human sacrifice in the first place; it was a test of Abraham's faith and love, which he passed with flying colors. But Dvora had talked about it as if it were her husband, her own Isaac. The idea of forcing Abraham to prove his love! What a paranoiac! (she really said that). Better Jesus Christ our Lord, a man-made God (her view), a cruci-fiction (her word), but at least He doesn't mess with your mind.

He turns on the ceiling fan, watches the blades pick up speed, rustling the pages of a book Dvora has left open. He thinks of their Isaac crying for his mother while she acts out her little tragicomedy. His anger is a fist pounding the back of his neck.

But understand, he tells himself. Dvora is smarter than you, has suffered more than you. Consider the messy, awful bundle of her loves and hates. Consider the effect of Muslim countries on the female ego. And the friend she lost to a bomb on a bus, a local bus on

the way to a movie in Tel Aviv. After that, she told
him, she wouldn't speak to her Palestinian friend or
answer his letters. But she still loves him, he knows;
she gets short of breath speaking of him. Thinking
about it he digs his nails into the palms of his hands
in order to stop thinking about it.

He's in the export business: dates, en route to a
meeting in Kuwait. English words roll around his
mouth like dates. He looks at her with his full face as
he talks, bathing her with his date-sweet breath. His
name, he says, is John West.

"John West—this is not true?"

He doesn't smile. His name is not a joke for them
to share. But he doesn't mind the baby's legs on his
lap as she changes him. He drapes her with his suit-
coat so she can nurse in private. She says, "You are
an angel of God."

"I, Missus, am a Christian."

She can't see him clearly on the dimly-lit train but
his whisper has the camaraderie of persecution shared.
She allows herself a series of regular breaths. On this
Arab train bound for a place she has never seen, John
West is understandable. Not an Arab because not a
Muslim (though she knows not all Arabs are Muslims). Perhaps an Arab but still a friend, cousin, a
young uncle (he is perhaps forty years old), his religion so much less different from hers than either from
that of their host country. "How is it," she asks, "to
be a Christian in this Muslim land?"

"Wonderful, yessiree. Fabulous to be a Christian."

His smile is awkward, like a skill learned late in life,
but presented, she feels, as a gift to her, along with the
fact that he went to university in the United States of
America. In the state of Texas, to be exact, the engi-

neering school of the University of Texas, although, sadly, circumstances at home compelled him to leave before he could receive his degree. He speaks quietly but rapidly, with the accent of people from the American West, about his business, the climate, the Kurds, the increasing prosperity of Iraq only temporarily slowed by the war, the fabulous hanging Gardens of Babylon, which she will be so pleased to see. Ike has gone back to sleep. She wants to sleep in the comfort of his pleasantly-conveyed general information.

But she cannot sleep. Outside the window on top of a small rise stands another portrait of President Saddam Hussein, his full figure, boots to military cap, the plywood or whatever it was painted on cut to his outline so that it casts a human shadow, more real for a moment than anything in the dim light of the train. John West, beside her, has moved from the Hanging Gardens to a description of Ur, where God first spoke to Abraham, and she sees Hussein's face before her, not cruel, just coarsely, powerfully whimsical, she wants to touch the dictator's close-shaven, fleshy cheek, the hard black hairs of his mustache. "A consecrated spot," says John West. "It holds much meaning in your religion."

"What is my religion?"

He whispers, "You are one-half Jewish."

She laughs harshly, clutching the remains of her secret of being a hundred percent Jewish, grandparents on both sides. "What else do you think you know about me? Where am I going?"

"To Kuwait. You have said, Missus, no?"

She cannot remember if she has said or not.

He goes on, "But you must not proceed all the way to Basra without stopping to see our fabulous national treasures of Iraq. The Hanging Gardens are perhaps not so beautiful as has been said, but Tall al-Muqqayar—You must visit the Royal Tombs, and the remarkable Ziggurat, where the moon god Sin has been worshipped, best preserved of ziggurats in the world, in Ur of the Chaldees where all of our remarkable religions began, I would be a *chump* if I did not accompany you."

"I plan to meet with my husband," she says.

"In the city of Basra?" he asks.

"In the capital city of Kuwait."

"Very good, yessiree," he says. "From Basra you must to Abadan to buy your ticket to Al-Kuwait, which train, I know, will not depart until tomorrow in the morning. It is the train I am myself taking. Please, Missus. Ur is very near to Basra, the very shortest ride by bus or taxicab from Ur to Basra, very much wounded in the tragic war but quickly repairing, where is my own small and poor apartment at your service."

"I have too few diapers—"

"In Basra are servants to wash for you. And still many beautiful hotels, with running water."

"Mr. West," she says, floundering for excuses though she is too proud for excuses. "My husband will be angry—"

"He will have no reason to be angry," he says, extending both hands to her, palm up. "He will be pleased for you to be traveling under protection in this country, no longer in the midst of an unfortunate war, but still sometimes unkind to foreign women. He will thank Mr. John West for showing you to Ur and then to Basra where my servant will make for you delicious American food. Missus would like a tasty American burger?" He smells not of dates but of sweet American aftershave, a gift, he says, from his American friend in Houston, Texas. He seems to have learned to speak from watching American cowboy movies, vocabulary, inflection. He is a sycophant, she thinks, an Americo-phile, for which she despises and then forgives him. To be a Christian among Muslims is like being a Jew among Arabs. She does not have to be afraid of him. She can feel perhaps superior to him.

"So it is agreed! Yessiree! You are hungry, Missus. Please to eat of my victuals."

He reaches down into the travel bag at his feet, takes out a small Thermos and opens it. The steam comes to her nose hot and strong.

"I have put much sugar," he says, "although I have more. Or perhaps first some treats from the market?"

He opens a paper bag, offers it. Dates and pistachios. She feels dizzy looking in the bag. Saliva fills her mouth. Her stomach squeezes.

"You are not hungry, missus?"

She swallows her saliva. Swallows again. She is very hungry. But taking his food is like signing a contract; in Hades she would not be allowed to leave. "We may not eat till sundown," she says, "while in Ramadan."

He laughs. "But you and I, Missus, we are not bound to the Five Pillars." He pours a cup of coffee. The train lurches. Coffee splashes her arm. "Missus," he says, "you must pardon our very poor trains of Iraq, rides most rough. If you will let me to assist you—"

He sets the cup on the floor between his feet and holds out his arms for baby Ike. Her skin quivers where the coffee hit but there is no other sensation. The smell of the coffee makes her throat ache. "Please, Missus," he says, "we must not drop this burning liquid upon his beautiful head. He is a boy, yes? A beautiful boy with such very white skin."

She puts her arms around Ike in his front pack, burying her nose in the fuzz on top of his head, but still she smells the coffee. Is coffee one of the exports of Iraq? Oil, dates and coffee. She hands Ike to the man beside her. He holds him upright, under his arms, talking into his face. Ike makes a happy baby sound.

John West seems gentler than Win, comfortable with children. She picks up the cup, orange plastic, as from a cheap lunchbox thermos. The coffee looks unutterably beautiful.

"Pardon me," he says, "but I see you are not liking my very good American Nescafé?"

It's hard to move her mouth even to talk. "I think they will throw stones at me."

"Nosiree," he says, pressing a couple of pistachios into a date and placing them in her half open mouth. "While journeying even the followers of Mohammed may eat food during daylight hours." He bounces Ike up and down, supporting his head so it doesn't bob. "Do not be afraid. Allah is not so cruel as many people believe."

He calls an American friend from the embassy. He does not tell his friend that Dvora and Isaac have been gone, how many hours? He tells him what a hard time Dvora is having in Baghdad. And that he plans to wind up his business ASAP so they can go where the folks are blond and pale, where she can get into a good argument in a language she likes. Dvora looks beautiful arguing, he says into the phone, describing her flushed face, her rapid breath, her voice almost breaking in the excitement of making a point. Hanging up he feels as if the top of his head is coming off.

In the mirror his face is serene. He looks harder for signs of madness, an aimless flicker of the eye. Dvora's crazy mother has a slight wobble in her walk, as if she doesn't trust the continuing power of gravity. Dvora walks like her father, as if she owns the streets and sidewalks, as if she made them, as if her will as she walks is just now laying the curbs and crosswalks.

This is the personal style he most admires, he
knows, based on the flashy wickedness of certain high
school friends (most of whom have since succumbed
to ordinary successes and failures, which still for some
reason doesn't diminish their attractiveness). It has
something to do with his response to Dvora. Right off
he was a little overwhelmed by her, by her unswerving
right steps, made right because of her belief in them.
Other people felt it too, her fierce self-assurance, rock-
hard, a little swaggering. When she talked, they listened; one of their college friends had confessed once
to being afraid of her, of her lack of fear. As if (the
friend had said this) she'd confronted something like
paradox, an overwhelming thing that wouldn't resolve
itself—she'd looked it in its multiple eyes and opened
her arms. He thinks: Or not exactly opened them, but
tried to and couldn't, couldn't but had to, kept on
trying to, and so couldn't look away from the whole
muddle of friends and enemies, terror and counter-
terror, her murdered friend and her sweet lizard,
whom she wouldn't speak to but whose picture she
kept, and all his letters.

He calls the operator, asks for the police. He misses
Isaac. He is tired of thinking about Dvora.

This is Ur, now Tall al-Muqqayar, where God con-
densed himself out of His cloud and ordered Abraham
to father His nation. She follows John West, though
the tarred road burns through the soles of her sandals,
though Ike's weight hurts her neck. She is thinking
about Abraham, seventy-five and childless, to whom
God said, Be fruitful and multiply. No fruit here now.
A couple of small houses near the railway station. The
land looks entirely barren, the color and topography
of a brown paper bag, although, according to John

West, 4000 years ago in the time of Abraham and Sarah, before the river changed its course, it grew rice and corn, dates and cotton, fertile and moist from the Euphrates.

"What made the river change course?" she calls out, unusual for her; she never asks questions. But she's a little dizzy in the heat, and her question is a link with the man who knows the way, whom she refused to let carry her baby. Her shoulders ache with the baby. Her purse hangs heavy from her arm. Her soles stick to the hot tar in the road, the thongs rub between her first and second toes, and she's so thirsty she has no saliva to swallow. This desert of asphalt and baked mud is hotter even than Baghdad, the heat deposited by the sun all day rising from the road to meet the heat still coming down from the late afternoon sun in what feels like a small, continuing explosion. The answer to her question shrivels into its separate words. At some point the road starts going uphill. At some point she passes through a gate in a chain link fence, but she's too tired to pay attention. She has no energy to give to anything but how to avoid the puddles of melting tar on the road, so she is almost upon it before she sees the ziggurat.

But this is not possible. It's too tall, too large not to have insisted itself upon her long before her eyes rose to its height. It must have materialized there on these rocks, this baked mud, while she was picking her way through the pools of tar, as she stopped for breath, as if wanting something larger than life was for once powerful enough to create it, rising before her wider than it is tall but almost too tall to bear, an idol so big she can't imagine the force that can smash it. Thirty centuries haven't been able to smash it though they've erased everything else on all degrees of the horizon— nothing else taller than a shack here. Not even a shack, just the framework of what might have been a

concession stand, now closed. She feels the impulse to
kneel and lets it pass, not even rejecting it, hardly conscious of it, the yearning for gods or idols, older than
Abraham.

"And this is only the first stage!" says John West as
if he had something to do with it. "In the time of the
Nabonidus, the last king of Babylon, it rose seven
stages, seven terraces, over 280 feet of sunbaked brick,
can one imagine?"

She shakes her head, though not at anything he
said. She remembers the painting of the Iraqi president
that she saw on the road to Babylon, now in her mind
like a big paper doll. Up ahead what seems to be a
flight of enormous steps leads to the top of the ziggurat. On either side two other long ramps meet at the
same point, though what is there she can barely see.

John West says, "On the seventh stage was built a
shrine to Nanna, the moon god, that was father to the
other gods, so these idolators believe. His name it was
also Su-en, nickname Sin. That is amusing, yessiree!"

His cowboy accent clashes, she thinks, with his
labored syntax. She walks away from him toward the
foot of the nearest staircase. He follows.

"Notice the lines," he says. "They appear straight
but in truth all curve inward, giving the eye the illusion of strength."

"Yes, of course." She puts her hand out and
touches the bottom step. The risers are much higher
than the treads are wide, as if the people who climbed
them had long legs with tiny feet. With Ike dangling
from her neck she begins to mount the ziggurat.

"Stop, please, Missus!" John West says. "It is not
permitted!"

"There's nobody here!" she calls back.

"You will hurt yourself. The steps go very high!"

"I'm not afraid of heights!"

"It is a national treasure of Iraq!" he cries, pleading. She hears tears in his voice. "It is a desecration."

But the *shamal* has stopped, the wind that blocks up her pores and her ears with its sound. And the sun is low on the horizon, the angle of light turning the pale brick golden. Coolness in the air gives her new energy. "I am a Jew," she calls back. "I am Israeli-American, what is to desecrate?" She keeps on climbing, out of reach of anyone's judgment. The steps are so high she needs her hands to heft her up, and her feet hurt, especially between the first and second toes, and occasionally Ike's head grazes the edge of a step, but she climbs rapidly and fearlessly, since heights have never bothered her and desecration has no emotional content. "I am an atheist!" she calls out. "I am not a follower of Sin!"

She yells down from the top of the ziggurat, not expecting any response, just to hear her own strong voice. At the gate in the fence surrounding the ziggurat she sees two men in uniforms the color of the desert. One of them smiles and waves at her. A dog is barking in the distance, a familiar, almost friendly sound. But John West is climbing after her. She feels stinging now on the backs of her arms, not from bug bites but the sun. And her feet, she sees, are bleeding, have been bleeding a while, some of the blood already dried a dark brown on the insole. There are bruises on two of her knuckles.

Do not wear sandals out of doors, she says to herself. Wear long sleeves.

The police are searching. They will call hospitals, hotels, train and bus stations, alerting officials throughout the city to a red-haired Western woman carrying a baby, easy to spot. He has heard the police of Baghdad are very good; efficient. He feels an almost idiotic relief.

These are the things he loves about Dvora: the way her features crowd together on her face, each demanding precedence. The way she calls him Mister America, not the name, which bothers him sometimes, but the way she says it, lingering over the R's as if she's making fun of his language and liking it at the same time. How much she loves the United States of America, not the politics, of course, but the idea, and the feeling on the streets, as fervently patriotic as he at nine singing the national anthem so loud his throat hurt and writing letters to Johnson against people who burned the American flag.

He goes into the kitchenette, warms coffee, pours sugar with a heavy middle-Eastern hand. Dvora appears in his mind as a warrior in handcuffs wrestling a warrior without hands, both so brightly sunlit he can hardly see them. When the light subsides to what the eye can tolerate, she's standing by him at the sink trying to cool her bug bites with water from the tap. She gives him a look of scorn and pity. She tells him how she felt for a moment, in an adopted country, something like peace, a series of tranquil moments. In American cities with their scramble of clothing, speech, ways of seeing, no one had reason to stare at her so she could sometimes forget herself. Walking along American streets she didn't have to think about her Palestinian lizard and her murdered friend and her awful Jewishness. He sees: On the Baghdad streets she was visible again, an object of attention, if not hostility, for anyone with the leisure to look at her. Over dinner once their educated upper-class host, who hadn't dined with them, told them with a voice of passion that a woman was a man's most treasured possession. And gazing down at baby Ike in her arms, she knew she couldn't be his mother without being his

Jewish mother, the means by which another Jew came to the fold, to be circumcised, bar mitzvahed and taught he was both better and worse than everyone else in the world, that he both deserved, ineluctably, inalienably, his Eretz Yisrael, that he had to inhabit it to stay alive, only to see his Jewish-Israeli relatives—they're all relatives descended from Abraham—behaving so hideously to preserve it he felt hideous himself, till his sense of decency (which might, of course, be just the old Jewish "kick me," the sheep's obedient crawl to the ovens) said to the enemy, *Ok, here, you take it if you want it so much.*

Is that puerile, Dvora Wallace née Blank? Is that amateur psychology?

The landing where the three stairways converge is rocky rubble with a few gray plants, the image, bounded and in miniature, of the ground below. The wind is utterly gone. The sun is gone too, vanished to red gold at the rim of the cloudless sky. Everything is cloudless, soundless, opaque blue, red and gold, a bowl of sky so hard the slightest sound or movement will crack it open. She doesn't move. A few feet in front of her and slightly above the level where she is standing is a rock the size of a steamer trunk, the only protuberance on the expanse of rocky plain that forms the second level of the ziggurat. There is no shrine, no second flight of stairs, nowhere else to go. Someone is screaming.

The sound seems to come from somewhere below, and she wants to run. But there is nothing to be afraid of, not John West, a Christian, as kind and helpful as he could be. Nothing to fear but her own irrational fear and hatred of this man who calls himself John West, although an Arab. She stands motionless, look-

ing at a single spot on the line where the sky and the
ground meet, when her companion's head emerges
over the rim of the stairs. She shrieks once, briefly. It's
the first sound she has uttered herself, separating her
from the awful noise, which comes—she looks where
he is looking—from baby Ike in his pack. He says—
sternly, she thinks—"He is angry, Missus!"

Ike is crying loud. His arms and legs are flailing, his
head whipping back and forth. She turns her back on
John West and touches her nipple to Ike's lower lip.
The noise stops all at once, as if sucked back into
where it came from. Ike smiles once, at the breast,
then seems to collapse around it, sucking in hard,
even tugs with his eyes closed.

"That is wonderful," says John West. "Yessiree.
And do you know, up here it is very nice, such a very
nice spectacular view!"

John West is looking at her as if she has performed
a miracle. A kind look, warm and respectful. Ike is
asleep in her arms, calm and rosy in the light from the
setting sun. John West spreads out his sportcoat in the
shadow of the large rock, and she sets Ike upon it,
stomach down. He continues to sleep. "It's an ordinary thing," she says. "Women do that." But she
feels proud of herself.

"Yes, of course, that is true. Do you know, I believe
that from here we can see to Basra!"

She walks over and stands slightly behind him. He
seems younger than she'd thought at first; whatever
lines she might have seen in his face are gone in the
dying daylight. Right now he looks not much older
than she. He is no taller than she. And inside his
bulky business suit he is slim, much slimmer than her
husband, frail, almost, like her lizard Ismal, Ismal
with the long thin face, who hated Israel but not most
individual Israelis, not *her*, she knew; who made her
tea on the three day march around Jerusalem, whose

bedroom walls were papered with Donna Summer posters, whose wide ribcage and almost hairless chest she can still feel sometimes between her hands.

"It is so very beautiful here," says John West. "I believe that if we build restaurants and handsome Sheraton hotels we may entice many Americans here to see it. But we are in troubled times now, and this peace is so very weak and frail, we will not build handsome hotels."

She kisses him on the lips.

There is no give but no resistance. It's like kissing a tree.

She does it again, harder, opening his mouth with her tongue. He pushes her away, but gently. He probably has Prince on the walls of his Basra apartment, she thinks, Cher behind Plexiglass. She can almost see the can of Nescafé in his cupboard, the bottle of American ketchup, and she feels tender toward him in a way she has never felt even with Ismal, tender and passionate enough to make love with him here on this desert island in the air while Isaac is sleeping.

But this is adultery, she knows, for which the Koran decrees death by stoning. She holds her breath for a moment, thinking of the Muslim punishment. In Pakistan it happened, deplored by lovely President Bhutto in her head scarf. But Win touches her so forcefully she has had to train herself not to flinch; it has been a long time since she wanted, really wanted, to make love with him. When the stones come for her she'll rise up in the air. Rocks will glance off her arms and the back of her head, touch her without harming. John West will touch her with questions in his small hands, the way a child touches a statue or an icon, something desirable and forbidden, forbidden because desirable, desirable because forbidden.

Ike starts to cry.

John West leaps away from her and kneels down beside the baby, who is crying louder than before, his back arching violently. She picks him up and offers her breast again. The crying stops, he sucks enormously hard three or four times—then he throws back his head, opens his mouth wide enough to swallow the sky and roars, flailing in her arms like a fish.

Her head feels full, as if the bowl of sky has suddenly closed upon it. She is overwhelmed by something that translates itself into itching on her skin, not in any bounded scratchable spot but up her arms and her legs, toward the narrow passageways to the inside of her. She knows what is wrong. Her milk did not come down this time with the baby's sucking. Cooing to Ike in her arms, she walks a circle around the flat rock at the top of the ziggurat. The heavy, dust-filled air makes her skin itch. She feels the tiny legs of Iraqi insects stepping through the tall grass of the hairs of her skin, insects so small they can crawl through mosquito netting, through openings in the weave of fabric, through her pores, she thinks, though she showered last night and this morning again with the prescription flea shampoo from the U.S. embassy doctor. She hasn't slept in six months with the itching, with the wondering whether each sensation was a new bite or an old itch or a figment of her sensory imagination, and she is so tired now, it's hard to know what to do about what has just begun to come clear, that John West wants her baby. That's why he has brought her to this isolated spot, she is suddenly sure—to take her baby with his beautiful white skin, his mark of the sun on his temple. Her beautiful white American baby so much more valuable than a trainload of dates, a woman's most treasured possession. But this is a very crazy thought. John West is innocent and kind. She must guard against thoughts like this in this country

so alien she can't look in anyone's eyes to see herself.
Ike keeps on crying.

"Perhaps he is overheated." John West picks his
jacket off the ground and starts fanning the baby with
a sleeve.

"Take that rag away!" she says.

The baby keeps on crying.

"Perhaps a small date," says John West, reaching
into his pocket.

"He does not eat solid food!"

"You may chew the date yourself, then deposit your
saliva into his mouth, that is not uncommon."

She pretends not to have heard him. The baby
keeps on crying.

"Perhaps he has received a bite or a sting. In this
land are many harmful insects. If you please, to place
him where we may inspect him." He spreads his
jacket out over the flat rock. "Here, Missus. There is
a slight declivity. He will not be able to roll."

The baby is bucking in her arms like a miniature
wild horse. Even in the twilight she can see that his
face is red. It gives off heat.

"Please, Missus—" John West tries to take Ike out
of her arms. She steps backwards, holding Ike firmly.
"I feel something," he says. "I believe there is a small
bite. Shuh, little baby. Shuh, little boy baby."

The crying subsides somewhat. She allows John
West to guide them over to the flat rock. He raises
Ike's shirt, smiling with a squint of the eyes, a widen-
ing of the closed mouth. "Yessiree. It is becoming
dark, Missus," he says, "but I have something from
America that is very useful!" He digs in his pocket.

"What is that?"

"It will be all right."

In his hand is something long and slim that gleams
in the dying light. Almost before she sees it she knows
what it is. And knows it's a test. Of her faith and

courage a test—that she will pass if she can place her son on the rock in front of John West. If she can open Ike's little blue shirt to the knife of John West, reciting the *Sh'ma* with her head bowed in obedience and faith: *Hear, oh Israel, the Lord our God, the Lord is One.*

But she has no faith, sees no sense in obedience toward anything but her own desiring. Or maybe it's Ike's shriek stabbing her brain that makes her whirl the child away from John West just as he's pointing out with his tiny penlight made in Dayton, Ohio, the small raised cap of an insect bite.

"Not poisonous, nosiree," he drawls, the line of smile widening his face, but knife or no knife, she sees beneath the smile and the business costume. He is an Arab, he is all Arabs, aflame with the righteousness of their cause inimical to her cause. Her body grows thick and strong, planting itself firmly on the crown of the ziggurat; it will not be pushed out of her country into any Mediterranean Sea. But he grows just as strong. They are equals in this place where their two nations were born. He is her one true husband.

The balance quivers a moment, precarious, lovely. Then her skin thinned by insect bites, or whatever sheath was keeping her parts together, begins to fray, to peel back, exposing to the dry air some raw terrified heart of her. She pulls her son off the altar of his sacrifice and runs for the stairway, the huge clay blocks of the stairs, the protection of the friendly guards, too fast to stop herself, her hands too full to grab onto anything, not that there is anything that can keep her from hurtling all the way down.

At first there was peace. It was as if a train had roared by. That's what he'd said to West, who'd seemed almost as shaken as he was; a fine person, West, the trouble he'd put himself to, bringing Ike back to Baghdad. There was peace. And there was Ike.

It remained true for a time even in this Israeli town of Herzliyya, even driving the multi-lane Israeli highway to Tel Aviv, where he will work for a while at simple sales distribution, not his old pioneering. It ran through his mind in Tel Aviv's rush hour traffic, in which he will spend a lot of time for the next few months. In the evenings when the *au pair* is off he'd spoon bananas into Ike's mouth and burp and change him, telling himself again and again: There is no one, nothing to blame but the ill-luck of birth and character and chance event, nothing anyone had control over.

But just when he thought he had the story down— she was a victim of her psyche and her history, besieged from inside and outside, doomed to fight to her death like the state of Israel (tragic, but what could anyone do?)—and he'd work mindlessly hard all day and sleep all the way through several nights in a row like Ike down the hall, then he'd have a dream in which he was walking through the rooms of a huge house. He'd go farther and farther in, living room to bedroom to rooms off rooms, which got smaller till he could no longer stand up in them. And he'd wake with a scream he'd try to hide from the *au pair*, thinking about what West had told him about the country in which he'd lived a year without knowing. Its president, who smiled at babies in his portraits but decreed death for anyone who made him the butt of a joke—the law a joke but on the books, said John West. Its mood of speechless terror, fear that cannot be voiced, what with informants at the bus stop, at the desk beside you, against not only Jews and

Christians but good Muslim citizens, who naturally wouldn't confide to him, a foreign visitor, what they couldn't say even in front of their children. Children who might be tortured to make their parents speak. A baby Ike's age deprived of milk, said John West, in the cell next to the cell where its father and mother sat hearing it scream.

On his good American double mattress in pretty little Herzliyya, named for Theodore Herzl who'd fathered the Jewish component of the Middle Eastern horror, he turns from his back to his stomach to his back again, knowing he missed it, the everyday murk those people were choking on. And guilt comes, or comes again, like a crab in the throat. In his two-bedroom apartment in this wealthy suburb of Tel Aviv (where there's a film studio, beautiful Jewish actresses; but why has he chosen to live among Jews?) he thinks about what else he missed, what West described to him, now so clear and bright before him in the night his eyes water to see it—Dvora holding Ike in her arms as she fell. What presence of mind, he says to himself. Heroic. Saintly, maybe. It had saved Ike's life. Then his mind bucks the reins of his reasoning and runs through the story all over again, what he said, she said, what he might have done if he'd known, if he'd known *her*.

Maybe next week when her parents visit (they come every Sunday, her father silent beyond weeping, her mother tremulous with presents for Isaac, carrier of the blood, the first grandchild and the last) he will ask them about Dvora. Because he didn't know her as he might have, as a husband ought to know his wife. Because no matter how many times he tries to imagine it he really can't say whether she held Ike so firmly as she broke herself in her fall down the stairs, out of a mother's love for her child above all else or her over-weening magical confidence that once they hit the ground she'd get up, zip him into his pack and carry him back to the station.

Contributors

CAROL ANSHAW's novel *Aquamarine* (1992) won the Carl Sandburg award and the Society of Midland Authors Award. She has also received the New York Book Critics Circle Citation for excellence in reviewing. Her reviews appear regularly in such publications as *The Village Voice Literary Supplement (VLS), Women's Review of Books,* and *The Chicago Tribune.* Her short fiction appears in such journals as *Story* and *VLS.* She is at work on a novel, *Seven Moves.*

ANNE BRASHLER's short story collection *Getting Jesus in the Mood* won the *Chicago Sun-Times* Best Fiction award in 1991. She is coeditor of *Storyquarterly* and of *The American Story: The Best of* Storyquarterly. Her writing has also appeared in *Chicago Works: Chicago Fiction, An Anthology,* and in a number of literary journals, including *New Letters, Cimarron Review,* and *Southern Humanities Review.*

JUNE RACHUY BRINDEL is the author of the novel *Ariadne,* which was nominated for a Pulitzer Prize; it was followed by *Phaedra* and the forthcoming *Clytemnestra,* as well as a collection of stories, *Nobody Is Ever Missing,* and a children's book, *Luap.*

MAXINE CHERNOFF has published five books of poetry, including *New Faces of 1952,* which won the Carl

Sandburg Award in 1985, and *Leap Year Day: New and Selected Poems*. Her story collection *Bop* is in the Vintage Contemporaries series. She is also the author of a novel *Plain Grief* (1991) and a second collection of stories, *Signs of Devotion*. She coedits *New American Writing* with her husband, poet and novelist Paul Hoover.

ELEANORE DEVINE is the author of *You're Standing in My Light And Other Stories* (1991), winner of the Friends of American Literature Award. She coauthored *The Dolphin Smile: Twenty-Nine Centuries of Dolphin Lore* with Martha Clark in 1967. She also publishes widely in journals such as *Kansas Quarterly*, *Southwest Review*, and *Indiana Review*, and has recently completed a novella.

JOYCE GOLDENSTERN's novella *Keeping Promise* won the *Quarterly West* competition in 1991. Her chapbook collection of stories, *Winter Grace*, was published in 1987. She contributes to journals such as *13th Moon, Other Voices*, and *Exquisite Corpse*, and is at work on a collection of fairy tales. Her nonfiction children's book, *In the Temple of Science: The Life and Work of Albert Einstein*, is forthcoming from Enslow in 1994.

MARY GRAY HUGHES is the author of two collections of short fiction, *The Calling* (1980) and *The Thousand Springs* (1971), and a novel, *The Empty Lot* (1992). "The Foreigner in the Blood" originally appeared in *Esquire* and was included in *The Best American Short Stories* of 1969. Her work has appeared in a variety of literary journals and anthologies. She is currently at work on a series of stories.

ANGELA JACKSON's *Dark Legs and Silk Kisses: The Beatitudes of the Spinners*, a book of poems, is forthcoming from TriQuarterly Press. Her other poems are collected in *And All These Roads Be Luminous*. Her play *Shango Diaspora: An African-American Myth of Womanhood and Love* is included in the anthology *Woman That I Am*, edited by Soyini Madison. Her fiction and poetry have appeared in many journals, including *TriQuarterly, Chicago Review*, and *Essence*, as well as in the anthologies *New Chicago Stories, Chicago Works,* and *Nommo: A Literary Legacy of Black Chicago.*

SANDRA JACKSON-OPOKU's work is included in the anthologies *Six Who Won; Say That the River Turns: The Legacy of Gwendolyn Brooks; Nommo;* and *South Side Stories;* and in journals such as *Heresies* and *Essence.* "To Those Who Come Behind Me" is excerpted from her recently completed novel in stories, *Songs and Daughters.* Her numerous fellowships and awards include the CCLM/General Electric Fiction Award for Young Writers, the International Film and TV Festival of New York Silver Medal Award and a National Endowment for the Arts Fiction Fellowship.

PATRICIA LEAR's short story collection, *Stardust, 7-Eleven, A & W, Route 57 and So Forth* was published by Knopf in 1992. She won an O. Henry Award for her story "Powwow" in 1991. Another story, "After Memphis," was included in *New Stories from the South: The Year's Best 1992.* She also publishes in *The New York Times Magazine* and *Chicago Magazine.* The recipient of fellowships to Yaddo and the Bread Loaf Writers Conference, she is currently at work on a novel.

SARA PARETSKY is the author of the bestselling series of V. I. Warshawski detective novels, including *Indemnity Only, Killing Orders, Deadlock, Bitter Medicine, Blood Shot, Burn Marks,* and *Guardian Angel. Deadlock* won the Friends of American Writers Award and *Blood Shot* won the Silver Dagger Award from the British Crimewriters Association. She was named Woman of the Year by *Ms.* magazine in 1988. She is a cofounder of Sisters in Crime, the organization for women mystery writers.

SHARON SOLWITZ is the fiction editor of *Another Chicago Magazine.* "The Country of Herself" was a runner-up in the Nelson Algren competition in 1992 (and published in *The Chicago Tribune*); she was also a runner-up in 1990. Her story "Dinner" was selected for the PEN syndicated fiction project in 1992. She has

published in such journals as *American Short Fiction,*
Ploughshares, Kansas Quarterly, and *Other Voices.* She is
at work on a novel.

DIANE WILLIAMS was a corecipient of the Pat Parker
Memorial Poetry Award in 1992. Her chapbook of poems,
The Color of Enlightenment, was published by New Sins
Press in 1991. Her poetry and fiction have appeared in
journals and anthologies, including *B City, Columbia*
Poetry Review, New American Writing, Common
Lives/Lesbian Lives, and *West Side Stories.* She is a
cofounder of *Kaleidoscope,* a journal devoted to works by
women of color.

S. L. WISENBERG has published stories, poems, essays, and
articles in *The New Yorker, Kenyon Review, Tikkun,*
Calyx, Another Chicago Magazine, and many others. She
has received fellowships from the Illinois Arts Council, the
Fine Arts Work Center in Provincetown, and the National
Endowment for the Humanities. She runs Red Fish Studio
Writing Workshop and is working on a novel.

About the Editor

KAREN LEE OSBORNE, a professor of English at Columbia College in Chicago, received her Ph.D. in English from the University of Denver. She was a Fulbright lecturer in American literature at Tbilisi State University in the Republic of Georgia.

She is the author of two novels: *Carlyle Simpson*, which won first prize from Friends of American Writers, as well as the Chicago Foundation for Literature Award in 1986; and *Hawkwings*, which was an American Library Association Gay & Lesbian Literature Award Finalist in 1992. She lives in Chicago, where she is working on a third novel.

Other Books from Third Side Press

FICTION

Hawkwings **by Karen Lee Osborne.** A novel of love, lust, and mystery, intertwining Emily Hawk's network of friends, her developing romance with Catherine, and the search throughout Chicago for the lover of a friend dying of AIDS. $9.95 1-879427-00-1

**American Library Association
1992 Gay & Lesbian Book Award Finalist**

On Lill Street **by Lynn Kanter.**

"Watching everyone struggle with her/his feelings, politics, impulses is truly engrossing and a joyful experience." —Bay Windows $10.95 1-879427-07-9

AfterShocks **by Jess Wells.** The Big One hits San Francisco. An 8.0 on the Richter scale and everything falls apart. $9.95 1-879427-08-7

"This book kept me up all night." —Kate Millet

Two Willows Chairs **by Jess Wells.**
Superbly crafted short stories of lesbian lives and loves. $8.95 1-879427-05-2

The Dress/The Sharda Stories **by Jess Wells.**
Rippling with lesbian erotic energy, this collection includes one story Susie Bright calls "beautifully written and utterly perverse." $8.95 1-879427-04-4

DRAMA

She's Always Liked the Girls Best **by Claudia Allen.**
Lesbian plays by two-time Jefferson-award-winning playwright. $11.95 1-879427-11-7

MYSTERY

Timber City Masks **by Kieran York.** Royce Madison tries her hand at sleuthing and is determined not to let bigotry take over her town. $9.95 1-879427-13-3

◢ Third Side Press

The book you are holding is the product of work by an independent women's book publishing company.

To order any Third Side Press book or to receive a free catalog, write to Third Side Press, 2250 W. Farragut, Chicago, IL 60625-1802. When ordering books, please include $2 shipping for the first book and .50 for each additional book.